# THE GORDIAN KNOT UNDONE

# THE GORDIAN KNOT UNDONE

## VALERIE BENZLEY

**FIVE STAR**
*A part of Gale, Cengage Learning*

GALE
CENGAGE Learning·

Detroit • New York • San Francisco • New Haven, Conn • Waterville, Maine • London

**GALE**
CENGAGE Learning·

**LIBRARY OF CONGRESS CATALOGING-IN-PUBLICATION DATA**

Benzley, Valerie.
    The Gordian Knot undone / Valerie Benzley.
       pages cm.
    ISBN 978-1-4328-2806-6 (hardcover) — ISBN 1-4328-2806-1 (hardcover)
    1. Antisocial personality disorders—Fiction. 2. Prisoners—Family relationships—Fiction. 3. Criminals—Rehabilitation—Fiction. 4. Parent and child—Fiction. 5. Psychological fiction. 6. Domestic fiction. I. Title.
PS3602.E7257G67 2014
813'.6—dc23                                    2013041015

First Edition. First Printing: March 2014
Find us on Facebook– https://www.facebook.com/FiveStarCengage
Visit our website– http://www.gale.cengage.com/fivestar/
Contact Five Star™ Publishing at FiveStar@cengage.com

Printed in Mexico
1 2 3 4 5 6 7 18 17 16 15 14

To my wonderful children, Nora and Ian. Your love and support keep me going.
To the Red Mountain Writers group. You guys rock!

# CHAPTER ONE

"Jessie—Jess Bell. Wake up. I need you. Something's wrong with the baby."

I sat up straight in bed, almost as though I'd been waiting for this. My mother stood beside me, cradling my little brother, Nathan. Her face looked like a mask in the dim glow of the nightlight—except for her eyes. They were glittering, the pupils dark and brilliant.

"Mama, what is it? What's wrong?" I marveled at how calm I sounded. "Give him to me. Let me see him." I held my hands out, cupped together as though she was just going to drop him in my arms.

"No. I've got him. I need you to run next door and call the hospital. Tell them he's not breathing."

My heart started pumping wildly in my chest. I choked out, "Mama."

She looked at me, her face completely expressionless. "I said I need you to get help. What are you waiting for?"

"Where's Matt? He could drive you to the hospital faster." My teeth had begun chattering as I pulled on my old gray sweatshirt over my flimsy pajamas.

She snorted. "Where do you think he is? Probably out drinking with those lowlife friends of his." She glanced down at the blanket-covered little body in her arms. "Now git! Hurry!"

I raced out of the house, the torn screen door slamming shut after me. The Estradas lived next door. They had a phone, not like us. They had a TV, too, and sometimes I was lucky enough to babysit for them. Those nights were like heaven—watching TV, eating the snacks Mrs. Estrada left for me, sitting peacefully on the couch. The kids usually went to bed right on time, and then the rest of the night was mine.

But right now all I could think about was the phone. The phone would save my brother. It would bring lights and sirens, medics and policemen. He would be okay, if I could only get to the phone.

Mr. Estrada opened the door to my frantic pounding. He blinked sleepily, clutching a plaid flannel bathrobe around him. "J-Jessie? What's wrong, *mija*?"

"It's Nathan, my brother, the baby," I screamed. "He's not breathing! He needs help! Help us, please!" I fell in a heap on the doorstep, sobbing uncontrollably.

Mr. Estrada gently pulled me up and ushered me into the house. "You sit," he said. "I'll call."

Mrs. Estrada came into the living room, sat on the sofa, and pulled me onto her lap. "Shh, shh, it will be all right." I was shivering and couldn't seem to stop.

I heard her husband on the phone, talking to the emergency operator. "Okay, Jessie, they are on their way. I'm going to see if I can help your mother." He turned toward the door.

"Mr. Estrada, no, don't go! I mean—" I knew my mother wouldn't want this kind, gentle man to come to the house. She didn't like the Estradas—didn't trust them. Sometimes she would call them terrible names, and laugh at me when I didn't join in. "Little Jessie wants to belong to a Mexican family. You'd have to change your name, y'know. They'd probably call you Conchita or something if you were their daughter. Better stick with your own kind, girl." I couldn't tell Mr. Estrada how she felt. My face was screwed up in a horrible grimace. He looked at me strangely.

"It's okay, *mija*. Listen, the sirens. They're almost here. Your mother needs friends right now." He walked out the door, tying his robe more tightly around him.

Mrs. Estrada began to rock me slowly and calmly. "Your brother will be all right, Jessie. He is a good, strong baby. The doctors will help him." Her voice was soothing and sweet, but it brought me no peace. I knew that my baby brother—my little Nathan—would not be all right. I knew he was dead when my mother woke me. And I knew that she had killed him.

My mother killed my father. Not only that, she also murdered my stepfather, my grandmother, and my baby brother. There, I've said it. Now, what do you think about me? Are you imagining that I must be a damaged, suffering mess of a person? Does it cross your mind that I might be a murderer in the making? Perhaps I've turned to prostitution or drugs to ease the pain of my unconventional upbringing.

You'd be wrong on all counts. I'm married to a wonderful man, I have three lovely children, and I work as a kindergarten teacher in our pleasant little town. I'm active in our church and have a wide circle of friends. Of course, none of the people in my life know about my mother. She remains my own private demon, my secret that I choose not to share—with anyone. My story is that my parents were killed in a terrible car accident when I was sixteen, and that the trauma of that experience so devastated me I prefer not to talk about it. I learned early that revealing as little as possible is usually the safest course.

So why am I telling my story now? Believe me, I've asked myself that question over and over. Maybe it has something to do with the fact that my oldest daughter is eleven. That was how old I was when I first started understanding that my mother was—different. Maybe it's because I'm due to hit that bugaboo milestone of forty on my next birthday. Or maybe—and if I'm to be totally honest, this is probably the only real reason—it's because of the letter I received yesterday.

My mother is being released from prison.

For over twenty years, I have presented myself as an orphan. I've done it so successfully that I often believe it myself. Occasionally something will bring a flash of remembrance to me—the scent of Pond's face cream, a quick glimpse of a blue Volkswagen, a red-haired woman crossing the street. I'm very good at pushing these memories down into the deepest hollow of my soul. Of course, giving birth to my children was a Herculean task all three times. It was all I could do to look at their tiny wrinkled faces and not be overwhelmed with grief for my baby brother. Thank God they were all girls. I don't know what might have happened if I'd had a boy.

A boy—little Nathan. He was the sweetest thing. Big brown eyes and a fuzz of dark hair. I was twelve when he was born, and he seemed like the perfect doll to play with. My mother spent a lot of time in bed after the birth—she said she was too tired to get up.

My stepfather was concerned, but he seemed to secretly love the opportunity her weakness gave him to bond with his son. He and I had the greatest time rocking him, tickling smiles out of him, and buying little boy clothes and toys. Nathan even had a football before he was six months old! Mama would stay in her bedroom, smoking and drinking endless cups of coffee. Matt, my stepdad, tried to talk with her about quitting smoking for the baby's sake, but he gave up pretty quickly. She had a way of looking at you—not saying anything, just staring—that made you back down without a fight.

Maybe I'm getting ahead of myself. Sharing this story for the first time is confusing, and even frightening. My thoughts are a complete jumble, and I pride myself on my calm and equable nature. I don't feel like myself anymore, and if I'm not myself, then who am I? Who am I?

"Begin at the beginning and go on till you come to the end: then stop." The King said that to the White Rabbit in one of my favorite books, *Alice in Wonderland*. It's good advice. I'll start at my beginning, and see where it leads.

# CHAPTER TWO

I was born in the dusty desert town of Needles, California. It's the kind of place people pass through. There's really nothing there to entice people to stay, unless they work for the railroad. My dad was a railroader. He was a cargo handler, and from what I remember he was typical of men with that job, big and burly. When he was home, the house was full of noise—sports on TV, friends stopping by for a beer, and most of all, the arguments.

He and Mama would start sniping at each other first thing in the morning and progress to knockdown drag-outs by evening. I was pretty young, but I can still remember huddling in a corner in my room, holding my favorite stuffed rabbit and trying not to listen. I'd tell stories to Bun-Bun about little girls who lived in beautiful gardens or in castles by the beach. I'd been to the beach once, on a rare family outing, and I fell in love with the mesmerizing sound of the waves.

Lots of kids grow up in contentious homes; it's not necessarily a recipe for disaster. What used to confuse me, though, was the way my mother could change her mood on a dime. One minute she'd be screaming obscenities at my dad, and then someone would call or come over and she'd suddenly—and I do mean suddenly—change into the sweetest, most refined person you'd ever want to know. She was the same way with me. Half the time it seemed as though she forgot I was even there—I learned how to make a peanut butter sandwich when I was barely three—and other times I was her "precious baby darling." I craved those times, and would do anything to get her attention. I remember brushing her red hair, telling her how beautiful she was. She would smile and pat my hand. "You're mama's baby girl. I can count on you. You and I will always be together."

I didn't know then what a life sentence those words meant.

I started school at Needles Elementary in 1981. There's a picture somewhere of me standing in front of our house wearing a plaid dress and bright white tennis shoes. I was clutching a Bionic Woman lunchbox. That show had been canceled, so Mama got the lunchbox at a discount. It's funny that I can remember the photograph so clearly, considering I'm sure I destroyed all of our family mementos long ago. As I recall, I had a somewhat anxious smile on my face. Even at age six, I knew that the best, most exciting experiences could suddenly turn upside down into chaos and anger. I'm guessing Mama took the picture, because my dad worked long hours. He usually left for work before I woke up and came home just in time to tell me good night.

It was sometime during that school year that things changed. My dad was home a lot more. The railroad boss told him he had to get his drinking under control, or he'd be laid off permanently. My mother was furious. She hated living in Needles, but it had been bearable when money was coming in. Now there was less money, and she was still stuck in a Podunk desert town. The screeching fights happened more often, and even got physical. Once my mama hit my dad with a frying pan, and he had to go to the emergency room. I remember that I was the first one to sign his cast, and I was so careful to print my name perfectly.

Of course, with everything going on at the house, I didn't dare invite friends home. At school, I'd usually go to the library after lunch, or stay in to help the teacher during recess. No one was mean to me, but they didn't pay attention to me either. I kept my head down and did my work. One thing I could count on was my mother praising me for good marks. "You're just like me, baby. We're smart—too smart for this godforsaken town. Things'll turn out for us, you'll see." Then she'd hug and kiss me, and I'd feel so warm and happy inside. But the next minute I'd be forgotten, her attention on some slight or insult she felt she'd received.

You see, it wasn't just my dad she'd get upset with. Neighbors, teachers, people at the grocery store—it seemed as though there were people everywhere who pushed my mama's buttons. Sometimes they used a "certain tone" when they spoke to her, sometimes it was "that look," and sometimes it was just that they seemed to be more educated or financially better off than my mama.

The worst thing I remember from those early years was going with Mama to my parent-teacher conference. It was just a routine visit to assess my progress and afford an opportunity for the parent and teacher to meet. I was excited and scared at the same time. Maybe my teacher would praise me, and Mama would be happy. But maybe she'd insult Mama, and things would get ugly. My heart was fluttering in my chest like a bat in a cave.

We walked into the classroom together, me half hiding behind Mama's full printed skirt, Mama striding in boldly as though she owned the building. The teacher, Miss Nairn, stood up as we entered.

"Hello, Mrs. Magruder. Hi, Jessie. I'm glad you could both come today."

I tried to sit very still, because Mama didn't like it when I fidgeted.

Miss Nairn sat down behind her desk. "I'm pleased to tell

you that Jessie is progressing quite well. She's one of the best readers in the class, and her spelling is also coming along nicely. Math is a little more of a challenge, but—"

Mama leaned forward, her eyes flashing. "A challenge? Is that a fancy way of saying you think she's dumb? My daughter has more brains in her little patoot than any of these other scummy lowlife idiots in this school. She's going to make something of herself. She's not going to end up being a poor-ass teacher someplace like Needles!" She sat back with a satisfied smirk.

Miss Nairn looked like someone had just set off a stink bomb right in front of her. Her mouth opened and closed but no sound came out. Finally she spoke. "Mrs. Magruder, I assure you I was not implying that Jessie is dumb. In fact, she's a very intelligent child. I am sure she will be successful in whatever field she chooses. I can tell you that, even at this young age, it's obvious she is college material."

Mama snorted and shook her red hair, whipping it back and forth. "Maybe you just think I'm dumb. Maybe you think you have to tell me what I want to hear so you won't get into trouble. I guess you don't know who you're dealing with, *Miss* Nairn. Never been married, have you? No kids of your own? You don't know how to get a man to do what you want."

My teacher just sat there, looking totally confused. I felt sorry for her. If I could have, I'd have given her a big hug and told her what a great teacher she was. But I just stayed still, trying not to breathe too hard, hoping that Mama wouldn't look at me. Somehow, I knew this whole argument wasn't about me at all.

"Come on, Jess Bell. We're going to the principal. I won't have you in a class run by someone like this stuck-up snob. We'll tell him how she's been treating you." Mama stood up and pulled me by the arm so quickly that I almost knocked over the chair.

Miss Nairn stood up, too. "Please, Mrs. Magruder, I'm so sorry if I offended you. I really enjoy having Jessie in my class. She's a delight." Her voice dropped to a whisper. "Please, Mrs. Magruder, this is my first year here. My job is important to me. Can't we work things out?" She held out a hand to my mother beseechingly.

I wanted to yell, "Don't say it! Don't let her see that you're scared! Now she's got you!" But I didn't say anything. I kept my head down, eyes on the brown linoleum floor, and followed Mama out of the room.

Mama marched us straight to the principal's office. His secretary tried to say that he was busy, but Mama said loudly, "Oh, I think he'll want to see *me*. You tell him Dolly is here. Tell him his old friend—"

The principal's office door was flung open before she could finish her sentence. Mr. Wilson, whom I was always in awe of, stood there looking flustered and embarrassed.

"Good to see you, Dol—I mean, Mrs. Magruder. And this must be little—" He looked pleadingly at me, silently asking for help.

"Jessie, sir," I whispered. He looked relieved.

"Of course, of course. What can I do for you, Mrs. Magruder?"

"There's a matter of deepest importance that I'd like to discuss with you." My mother moved closer to the principal, a worried look on her face. Her voice had just a hint of a southern drawl. I'd never seen her look more beautiful.

He turned to his secretary. "Wanda, hold my calls. This is a private meeting."

I slumped down in a chair outside his office. I wondered why I'd never noticed before how often Mr. Wilson repeated his words. I wondered which class my mother would get me moved to. And most of all I tried not to wonder about what my mother and the principal were doing behind that thick oak door. I'd seen the way he looked at her, and how he'd put his arm around her shoulders as he ushered her in. I started singing a song in my head that Miss Nairn had taught our class so I wouldn't hear the faint giggles and voices coming from the office. "This little light of mine, I'm gonna let it shine, Let it shine, Let it shine, Let it shine."

# CHAPTER THREE

Mama got her way. It was no surprise to me. After what seemed like a long time, she and Mr. Wilson came out of his office. They were both laughing. She stopped at the door to reapply her lipstick, and he touched her arm.

"You don't need that. You're beautiful just the way you are." His eyes had a hungry look.

"You are just so sw-e-e-e-t," she replied, drawling out the word. She had that super-excited, manicky expression on her face that I had come to dread. It meant unexpected things would be happening, and unexpected in my experience usually meant bad.

I saw Mr. Wilson's secretary looking at the two of them with disgust. She had light-colored glasses with an old-fashioned cat's-eye design. They glistened in the overhead fluorescent lights. Then she glanced at me, and her expression changed to one of pity.

I was having none of that. I quickly jumped out of my chair and grabbed my mother's arm.

"Come on, Mama," I said in an unnaturally loud voice. "Daddy should be home by now."

Mr. Wilson had the grace to look embarrassed, but Mama shook my hand off her arm viciously.

"Now, darlin', what are you talking about? You know your daddy is working late today. We have all the time in the world— just you and me tonight." She glared at me, all the more terrifying because she did so with a smile on her face.

I lowered my head. "Sorry, Mama."

"And I want you to give Mr. Wilson a great big thank you. He's moving you out of that nasty old Miss Nairn's class and in with someone who knows how to teach such an extraordinary child as you."

I raised my head and stuck out my hand to shake with Mr. Wilson. "Thank you, sir."

"And I don't think Miss High-and-Mighty Nairn will be here at this school much longer—will she, Johnny?" She turned back to the principal, smiling broadly as though they shared a private joke.

"Well now, Dolly, I will definitely be keeping a close watch on her. You know there are procedures to be followed—these gosh darn unions."

Mama stuck out her lower lip, pouting prettily. "But Johnny, you promised!"

"Don't you worry about a thing, my dear. And as for you, young lady, I think you'll find Mr. Finicelli is an outstanding teacher. Why, he has requests every year from parents desperate to get their children into his class."

I nodded, but inside I felt like crying. Miss Nairn had always been so kind to me, and she loved reading as much as I did. Mr. Finicelli was always taking his class out to the playground for boisterous games of dodgeball.

With a final gushy farewell, Mama and I swept out of the office. Or rather, she swept and I was just borne along. When we got to the car she stopped abruptly and put both her hands on my shoulders.

"You do not defy me," she said in measured tones. "You do not embarrass me in front of my friends. Do you understand?" She spoke softly, but her nails dug into my skin through my cotton blouse.

"Yes, ma'am." When Mama was in this kind of mood, it was best to speak with extra respect. I prided myself on not flinching as her nails penetrated deeper into my flesh.

She opened the passenger door and shoved me inside, then swung around the car and got in behind the wheel.

"Okay, precious darlin'," she sang out. "Let's go have some fun! Want to go shopping?" Her green eyes glittered like there were little fireworks going off inside. She smiled broadly.

"I don't need anything, Mama. You don't have to spend money on me."

"Of course you don't *need* anything, silly-billy. Shopping is about getting what you *don't* need." She laughed uproariously and tickled me.

I couldn't help laughing, too. It was fun to feel like we were on an adventure together. Maybe this time it would have a good ending. Maybe this time Mama would stay in her happy mood, and she'd be proud of me.

We pulled into the parking lot of Woolco. Needles didn't have much in the way of shopping, but you could get anything you needed at Woolco. I loved going there, because they had soft-serve ice cream at a little counter in the back.

"Can we get ice cream, Mama?" I asked timidly.

"Since when have we ever come to Woolco and not had ice cream? You can even have a double cone if you want. But first we're going to do some heavy-duty shopping. We'll get our ice cream after that, so it won't melt all over our pretty things." She laughed again, and I joined in, feeling all the unhappiness of earlier in the day flying away.

"You know, some people are saying Woolco is going to be going bankrupt soon," she confided as we got out of the car and walked toward the store. "I swear, if that happens, there won't be *any* reason to stay in this stinky old town." She pulled me by the hand. "Hurry up now, we have some money to spend!"

I wasn't sure what bankrupt meant, but it didn't sound good. And I'd miss Woolco, too, if it went away. I imagined a giant bank falling from the sky on top of the store. Maybe it was something like that.

But I had no time to wonder about word meanings. We were in the store, and my mother was heading straight for the jewelry counter.

"Oh darlin', just look at these pretty earrings! They just match my eyes, don't they?" She held up a pair of glittery green hoops next to her ears.

"They're beautiful, Mama—just like you."

She gave me a quick hug and whispered breathlessly in my ear. "Just put 'em in your pocket, darlin'. Do it quick now."

I obeyed. It wasn't the first time Mama had enlisted me in her Robin Hood scheme. That's what she called it—Robin Hooding. We were just taking from the rich to give to the poor. It wasn't stealing, it was just righting a wrong.

Then it was off to women's wear, and then the children's department. We had so many articles of clothing that we had to get two carts. Shoes, purses, perfume—all went into the steel maws of the shopping carts. It felt like we were on one of those TV game shows, where you got to pick as many things as you wanted from a store in just a few minutes. We were literally racing from department to department. Mama kept me laughing with her running commentary on the other shoppers.

"Jess Bell, look at that one over there," she'd whisper. "Doesn't she look just like that big pink pig on the ad at the grocery store?" I'd look, and we'd both dissolve into giggles.

Finally it was time to check out. Mama expertly scanned the registers, getting in line at the end one.

"Mama, this line is lots longer than the other ones. Don't you want to move one over?"

"Shush now. I know what I'm doing. Just watch me work."

After an interminable wait, it was our turn at the register. As I looked up at the clerk, I understood Mama's plan. He was a homely, skinny man with a big mole on the side of his nose.

"Did you find everything you needed—whoa, I guess you did!" When he smiled he looked much better.

"Sure did, sugar. I just lo-o-ve this store," said Mama in silvery tones. "I swear, if Woolco goes out of business, I don't know *what* I'll do! You all are always so courteous and professional." She smiled and looked up at him through her thick eyelashes.

"Why, thank you, ma'am." He actually blushed.

"Oh, don't call me ma'am—that makes me feel so old! Now, let me just find my checkbook—here it is! Honestly, if my head wasn't attached—well, you know." Her tongue licked her lips, just the tiniest bit.

I scrunched down, trying to be as small and unnoticeable as possible. I knew what was coming next. It had happened before.

"Let me see—oh my Lord! I can't find my ID! I'm sure I put it in my purse this morning! Jessie, Jess Bell, were you playing with Mama's ID again?"

"No, ma'am," I mumbled. Apparently I hadn't made myself small enough.

"That's okay, ma'am—I mean, miss. I guess this one time I can accept a check without ID. After all, I am the assistant manager." He beamed with pride.

"Aren't you just the sweetest thing?" Mama's voice went up an octave. People in line behind us were starting to shift from foot to foot, looking disgruntled. Mama didn't seem to notice. Her attention was on the clerk.

"No problem, miss. Now, I'll just take that and—uh-oh." His face took on a look of anxiety.

"What is it? Did I put the wrong date on it or something? I'm such a silly goose sometimes."

"Ma'am." He leaned forward, and spoke in an undertone so the people behind us couldn't hear. "I'm afraid we can't take this check. It's on our list."

"List? What list?" Mama's eyes opened wide, her face the picture of innocence.

"Bad check list," he mouthed, trying to not to humiliate her in front of a crowd.

"I have never been so insulted in all my life!" My mother seemed to grow taller and bigger with indignation. "I should have known better than to shop in this dirty little store, especially when it's run by people like *you*. You might think you're a high and mighty manager, but let me tell you—you're nothing but a sad little clerk, working a sad little job. Come on, Jessie. We're outta here."

She grabbed me by the upper arm and marched me out the door, leaving our pile of treasures on the counter. I made the mistake of looking back, and wished I hadn't. The man stood there with a stricken look on his face, as if he'd just been bitten by a snake. I knew just how he felt.

My stomach was tied up in knots. I told myself it was because it had been expecting ice cream and been disappointed. I was pretty good at pretending, too.

# CHAPTER FOUR

I'm having a hard time dealing with this next part. It's more difficult than I thought, remembering the scared little girl I used to be. And things have been crazy in my life lately. That's funny—crazy. My life now is really so much less crazy than anything I experienced growing up. It would be more accurate to say that I've simply been under some stress. And stress is something I know how to handle.

It's just that everything seems to be happening at once. My oldest, Amelia, is struggling with integers. She's in fifth grade, and it seems as though she's not taking her education seriously. I've tried to explain to her that her poor performance reflects badly on me, both as a parent and an educator, but she just looks at me with a blank stare. She's not normally a defiant child, but I'm beginning to wonder if she really cares what I think.

The two younger girls are still so sweet and cuddly. Amanda is six, and Abigail is five. I love hugging them and smelling their freshly washed hair. I always use baby shampoo on them. You can't be too careful about additives and dyes in products. Baby shampoo is clean and pure, like them.

Work has definitely added to my pressure lately. When I first started teaching, I loved kindergarten. The children were so innocent and eager to learn. They would often bring me little crayoned pictures of me as a princess, or flowers from their mothers' gardens. They loved listening to me at story time. I felt like I was truly shaping them, molding them into decent, honorable people.

But the last few years have been different. Children today seem to have a pseudo-maturity that is frightening—even ugly. The girls dress like little tarts, and the boys are aggressive and unruly. Sometimes, by the end of the day, my face actually aches from forcing myself to smile calmly. It's important that I remain in control, because otherwise who knows what might happen?

Most troubling of all is my relationship with Dan, my husband. He used to put me on a pedestal, as though I were made of fragile china. He was so solicitous of my feelings, rubbing my feet after work, running me bubble baths, even cooking dinner at least once a week so that I could have some alone time. He was the perfect husband, and we had the perfect marriage.

Lately, though, he has become impatient and abrupt. If I try to talk to him about work, or Amelia's bad attitude, he brushes me off and changes the subject. He's been working late most nights and when he comes home he barely acknowledges me. Sometimes I've caught him pouring himself a scotch before going to bed. He knows how I feel about drinking, so all I can assume is that he just doesn't care. He's obviously more concerned about himself and his needs than those of the children and me.

And then, of course, on top of everything, there's the letter. I can't believe they're releasing her. I don't care how old she is (and she's actually ten years older than I thought she was, growing up)—the woman is a danger to society. At least I've been warned. I don't think she'll have any way to find me—the prison system is pretty good about protecting victims' identities. My name is different, and I live on the other side of the country from where she was convicted. I've built a new life—a good life—and she can't hurt me. Her power is gone.

So why do I feel so tense and upset? Why do I find myself snapping at the girls—even my two precious babies? I need to find some way to regain my equilibrium. I can't let her win again.

It would be easier if other people would cooperate. It's bad enough that members of my own family are starting to turn against me, but even people on the periphery of my life seem to be opposing me.

For example, at the grocery store the other day, I was in the express line behind a woman who had more items than were allowed—and on top of that, she wrote a check! I mean, really, how inconsiderate can some people be? You only go to the express line because you're in a hurry. I spoke sharply to her and told her just how rude and self-centered she was. She actually rolled her eyes at me! I was just about to tell her how childish and silly she was behaving when the clerk—the clerk!—told me to calm down or go to another register. A woman with probably no more than an eighth-grade education telling me, an educated woman, what to do. I walked out of that store and I plan on never returning. I held my head high and kept my dignity. I couldn't resist shoving my cart into that odious woman who started the whole mess. She yelped like a hurt puppy, but I didn't look back. People like that don't deserve the time of day.

I think what I need is some time alone. I need to restore my sense of serenity, my calm center. Things seem to be spiraling out of control, and I need to take charge before the whole situation gets any worse. In the old days, Dan was so attuned to my feelings that he would have nipped this unholy mess in the bud. He would have bought me something pretty, or told me to lie down with a cold cloth on my forehead while he saw to the girls and the housework. He might have even urged me to spend a whole day doing whatever I fancied—a spa trip, a day at the shore, or just a little shopping spree.

Well, those days are gone, and I've never been one to cry over the past. What's done is done, and you have to move on. If Dan doesn't want to take care of me anymore, I'll just have to take care of myself. I think a weekend at that little boutique hotel upstate might just do the trick. Dan and I went there last year for our anniversary, and it was just so delicious. Everything was perfect—the single red rose in the vase by the bed, the gourmet meals, the tender care provided by the staff.

Dan has been complaining about bills lately, but I think he's just trying to scare me. Sometimes he acts as though I'm another child instead of an intelligent, praiseworthy woman. The joke's on him—I know where he keeps his "secret" credit card. He thinks I don't know about it, after he cut up our other cards in front of me last month. I knew he'd keep one card out of the mix, and he did. He really should know better than to try and outwit me. I booked a single room that same day for a two-night stay. Anything more than that would be self-indulgent. I can't miss work, and I don't want to be away from the girls for too long. My husband seems to be a competent parent, but nothing can make up for a mother's care.

When Dan got home that night—late as usual—I greeted him with a smile and a kiss. I microwaved his cold dinner and served it to him on our best china. He seemed confused, but it didn't take him long to relax. He actually got a little chatty, boring me with some long story about his work. I mean, how exciting is it to be a dentist? Looking in people's slobbery mouths all day—ugh. It was something I'd really had to work on when we were first married. I know it's great security to be married to a professional man, but I'd hoped for something a little more refined, like law. Of course, Dan had tricked me, and we ended up in wedded bliss before I knew it. Back then, I was his everything.

"Honey," he said hesitantly. I brought my attention back to the present.

"Yes, sweetie, what is it? Are you ready for some dessert? I have your favorite ice cream." I kept my voice light and lilting.

He reached out and grabbed my hand. "No, that's okay. It's just—tonight you seem like your old self. I've missed you."

I smiled, my big kindergarten grin. "Danny, you're so silly. I haven't changed. I'm still your same little sugar pie."

He grimaced slightly and shook his head. "I can't believe I used to call you that. It's so corny."

I felt a little spark of anger inside but quickly quenched it. "Danny, I love our little pet names for each other. Don't tell me you've outgrown them." I opened my eyes extra wide.

With a sigh, he let go of my hand. "Thanks for dinner. Maybe I will have some of that ice cream before I hit the sack."

"One dish of vanilla bean, coming right up. Want some sprinkles on that, or a cherry on top?"

Dan's voice was oddly flat as he replied. "No, that's okay. Just plain vanilla is fine."

In the kitchen, I quickly crushed an Ambien and stirred it into the ice cream. Hmm—maybe two would be better. Yes, better to be safe than sorry. The taxi would be picking me up in just a few hours, and I needed to be sure Dan would sleep tight while I made my escape. I giggled a little to myself. Tomorrow morning I'd be waking up in a beautiful, fluffy white bed, ordering room service. Meanwhile, poor old Danny boy would be dishing up the cereal and combing the snarls out of three little girls' hair. I looked critically at the ice cream in the bowl. Thank goodness he liked vanilla bean. The texture should mask the Ambien nicely.

"Here you go, sweet thing. Eat up." I beamed while he picked up his spoon and dug in.

# CHAPTER FIVE

I stretched luxuriously in the soft white sheets. Glancing at the clock, I saw that it was nine thirty. I hadn't slept that late in years—not since the children were born, anyway. A smile crept over my face. Right about now Dan would be trying to get Amelia ready for her music lesson, while simultaneously getting the two little ones presentable for the day. Amelia always dragged her feet about going to piano lessons. She didn't realize how lucky she had it. I would have killed for the chance to study music and have a loving mother and father. She really was very ungrateful.

I reached for the phone. I had turned my cell off last night, because I knew Dan would call once he woke up and found me gone. I waited while it rang.

"Hello—Jess, is that you? Where are you? Are you all right?" His voice sounded suitably distraught.

I didn't say a word. He continued to jabber frantically. I held the phone away from my ear until he paused.

"I'll be home Sunday afternoon, sweetie. Don't worry about me." I gently hung up the receiver to his irritating squawks.

After an elegant room service breakfast—eggs Benedict, fresh-squeezed orange juice, and a homemade muffin—I took a long restorative shower. This was the way I was meant to live. I deserved to be treated like a queen. I frowned slightly as I scrubbed my elbows with the loofah. Why did that phrase seem so familiar? Of course—Mama used to say the same thing.

"But I am not her," I said out loud as I dried myself with the thick fluffy towel. "I am nothing like her."

I poured myself a second cup of coffee and went out to the balcony. The view was fantastic. My room overlooked the English-style garden, which was a riot of color and perfume. Somehow I couldn't fully enjoy it. There was a niggling little something at the back of my mind. That letter! It was ruining my secret escape. I shut my eyes, and remembered.


After Mama and I got home from the store that day, I went straight to my room. I knew she was spoiling for a fight, and I didn't want it to be with me. She'd been muttering to herself on the drive home, punching her fist into the steering wheel as she drove. I knew better than to try and talk. I just hoped to stay invisible.

Sure enough, when Daddy came home, she laid into him right away. He'd barely walked in the door before she started.

"You have got to be the biggest loser in this town! You can't even manage to make enough money for the bare necessities for your wife and daughter! Why did I ever hook up with you? I should have known someone named Earl would be nothing but a stupid flunky!"

"Whoa, Dolly. What's going on? What the hell are you talking about?"

She snarled like an angry wolf. "I'm talking about your pathetic job and your lack of manhood. Only a sissy-boy would put up with going to work every day at such a dead-end, nothing job." I heard a crash. She'd probably thrown an ashtray at him, but I knew he was a pro at ducking.

"Look, babe, it's been a long day and I'm too tired to fight. Lemme get a beer and then we'll sit down all calm and find out what this is all about." His footsteps sounded as he went into the kitchen. Our floors were pretty squeaky.

But he wasn't going to get off that easily. She followed him, her voice getting higher and screechier. I crept into my closet and shut the door, just leaving it open a crack. I started singing to myself so I wouldn't hear them.

I must have fallen asleep, because when I woke up it was dark. I sat up and rubbed my eyes. What was that noise? It was a thump, and then a drag, another thump, and then a drag. I listened more intently, and breathed a sigh of relief. I could hear my mother, cursing under her breath. If she was out there, that must mean it wasn't a bad guy making those noises.

I left the closet and stood in the doorway of my room. "Mama?" I asked, feeling like a baby. "Are you okay? What's wrong?"

She turned and glared at me, her eyes shooting out electric sparks. She'd been pulling some sort of big package, all wrapped up in sheets and garbage bags.

"Get back in bed, Jess Bell—now!" She hissed the words, making them seem scarier somehow.

"But what is that? Can I help—"

She reached out and slapped me across the face. I put my hand up to my cheek, blinking back tears. I knew better than to cry.

"Don't argue with me, girl. Git!" She leaned down and started tugging on the unwieldy bundle. I moved backward into my room, not taking my eyes off of her. Somehow I knew this was something I needed to remember.

I didn't sleep much that night, but I must have dozed off at some point. When I woke up, I could hear Mama singing in the kitchen. It surprised me that she was up and making breakfast. Usually I poured my own cereal and milk and ate alone.

"Gonna wash that man right outta my hair, gonna wash that man right outta my hair, and send him on his way." She turned as I entered the room.

"Good morning, sugar plum. How'd you sleep? No bad dreams or anything?" Her mouth was smiling, but her eyes weren't. She twirled the spatula in her hand. "Ready for some pancakes?"

"Yes, please. Do we have syrup?" I sat down at the table.

"Sure do, snugbug. We've got everything we need, now." She turned back to the stove. "But before you get your goodies, you gotta help Mama. Be a sweetie pie and put those dishes away, now."

I looked over to the dish drainer. There wasn't much there, just a few glasses and saucers—and the butcher knife. What had Mama been cutting up? I wondered. Pancakes didn't need chopping. I shrugged and got the dishtowel, making sure everything was really dry before I put them away.

"Mama—Mama—where's Daddy? Is he working today?" I felt brave when I was addressing my question to her back.

"Oh darlin'—I don't know how to tell you—but Daddy's gone. He left us, without a single thought. He didn't really care about us, Jess Bell. We're better off without him." She made a sad face and turned back to the pancakes, humming slightly as she flipped one and put it on a plate.

I sat silently, thinking. Thinking about what I'd seen last night. Thinking about how the kitchen floor looked all shiny and clean. Thinking about the big butcher knife, freshly washed in the dish drainer.

"Ready for a perfectly beautiful pancake, darlin'?" Mama stood over me with a plate in her hand.

"Yes, ma'am. You are the best mama ever. I love you so much."

She set down the plate and gave me a big hug, squeezing me so tight I could barely breath.

"It's just the two of us now, Jess Bell. We're together through thick and thin. Don't you forget it."

I hugged her back.

# CHAPTER SIX

I looked out of the cab's back window as we drove away from my sweet little retreat. Sunday had come all too soon, and now it was back to reality. I settled against the seat and sighed. It wasn't that I didn't love my family—in fact, my arms were aching to hold my two little ones—but it had been wonderful to just think about me for a change.

I must have nodded off, because before I knew it the cab had stopped and the driver was saying, "Ma'am? Ma'am? We're here." I blinked and dug in my purse for that handy-dandy little credit card. I gave him an extra-big tip.

As I walked up our brick walkway, I felt like I was in a daze. That was my house, those were my roses lining the walk, but where was my family? Where was Dan, rushing out to meet me? Where were my girls?

When I got to the door, it was locked. How humiliating! Locked out of my own house! I grabbed my keys and opened the door. "Hello, Mama's home. Come out, come out, wherever you are." They were probably hiding to surprise me, I thought. But no one answered.

I tossed my keys onto the entry table, and that's when I saw the note.

*"Jess—we're at Mom's. Call me there. Dan."*

I crumpled the paper and threw it across the room. A throbbing started in my head, right behind my left eye. "No-o-o-o!" I howled. Running into the living room, I grabbed the ugly figurine his mother had given me for my last birthday. It made a satisfying crash as I hurled it against the fireplace. I started looking for something else to destroy, and suddenly caught myself.

"You're not like her, you're not like her. You are calm, intelligent, in control. You're not like her." My breathing slowed as my mantra soothed me. I sank down onto the couch and picked up the phone.

His mother answered. "Oh, Jess, we were so worried ab—"

"May I speak to Daniel, please, Mrs. Stranahan?" My voice was calm but icy.

There was silence, then Dan got on the phone. "God, Jess, where did you go? What have you done? Do you have any idea of what this escapade of yours did to the kids—to me? What the hell did you think you were doing?"

I knew Dan must be really angry to swear like that. He's normally so gentle and considerate.

"Dan, sweetie, please let me explain. Come home and we'll talk about it. I miss you and the girls so much," I choked up a little, and I wasn't just pretending. I really did miss them.

"We have a lot to talk about, all right. Like why you took off without a word, and where you got the money for your little fling. But mostly, I want to know why you're getting letters from Nevada State Penitentiary. What are you involved in, Jess? What's happened to you, to our life? It's like I don't even know you."

I froze. "Wh-what did you say?"

"I said, what's going on? Who or what are you involved with? I need the truth, Jess."

"Someone's trying to cause us trouble, Dan. They're spreading lies about us. That's why I had to go away for a while. I was supposed to meet with this woman—an evil, evil woman, Dan—who's trying to destroy our family. But then when I got there, she never showed up." My words came out faster and faster. "Please, baby, please come home. I'm so scared." Now I was crying in earnest.

"What? What are you talking about? Jess, don't cry. Calm down. I'll be right there. Maybe I should leave the girls with Mom for awh—"

"No!" It came out like a shout. I stopped and took a deep breath. "We need to be together, Dan. We can't let them out of our sight. I'll explain everything. Just please hurry."

I put the phone down, my mind racing. I hadn't lied, not really. There *was* an evil woman who wanted to destroy us. Dan just didn't know it was my mother, and he never would know, as long as I still drew breath. Now, how could I lay this out for him so it would sound plausible? I could do this—my IQ was the highest of all the students at Maddock High. In fact, I was pretty sure it was higher than Dan's.

By the time I heard the minivan pull into the driveway, I was ready. I flew out the door, dabbing at my eyes with a lace handkerchief.

"Dan! Babies! Oh, how I missed you! Come here and hug me! I need your hugs!"

Dan and the two little ones ran into my arms, all of us crying. But something was wrong. I looked over Dan's shoulder.

Amelia stood on the front step, not saying a word. She hadn't run to me, telling me she missed me. She wasn't crying. Our eyes met. I looked away first.

Dan ordered pizza, telling the girls it was a "Mommy welcome home" treat. I didn't protest, even though usually I didn't allow them to eat such greasy food. We both bathed them and put them to bed, reassuring all three that everything was fine and they would be safe. Amanda and Abigail reached up to kiss me good night, smelling so sweet and clean. Amelia turned her face to the wall.

"I know you're upset, darling," I said gently, stroking her hair. "But Mama's here now, and I won't go away again."

She didn't answer.

Dan and I walked into the living room, our arms around each other. This was the moment of truth. My husband had to believe me—he had to. Our family was in danger, and we could only combat the enemy by holding fast together. I remembered how he'd caved when I was crying, and felt stronger. He wouldn't let me down.

He sat on the couch and I snuggled up next to him. I gently kissed his cheek. "Oh Dan, I'm so glad we're together. I want to tell you everything. I've—I've been so scared, sweetie." Tears sprang into my eyes.

He put his arm around me and pulled me closer. "Jess, we're a couple—man and wife. Whatever the problem is, we'll face it together. Now, just start at the beginning and tell me what's going on."

I took a deep breath, stifling the urge to laugh. Start at the beginning? I don't think so. The last thing I wanted Dan to know was anything about my origins. Instead, I started with something he could accept.

"Dan, you know how involved I am in charity work. Well, someone at school told me about this prison ministry. I thought it wouldn't hurt if I wrote some poor woman a letter of encouragement—you know, it seemed the Christian thing to do. It was such a little thing I didn't even mention it to you. Of course, you've been working so much, we don't talk like we used to."

I sneaked a look over at him. He was hanging his head, obviously feeling guilty. Good. This was going perfectly.

"Anyway, the next thing I knew, she was writing demanding letters, full of horrible threats. I didn't respond, but it was obvious she had talked with someone who was acquainted with us.

She knew too much. She even mentioned the girls by name! I was so scared, Dan! I didn't know what she might be capable of doing!" Tears flowed down my face and choked my voice. I cried more freely, imagining how awful such a situation would be.

He took my face in both of his hands, so gently and lovingly. "But Jess, why didn't you tell me then? Why did you try to handle this on your own?"

"Baby, you've been so worried about your practice. I know losing Dr. Folgate was a blow. I just didn't want to add to your stress. After all, I was responsible for getting us into this mess. So when she called and said she was getting released and wanted to meet with me, I guess I just panicked. I thought I could find out what she wanted and appease her somehow. Oh Dan, I've been so stupid! I should have told you right away!"

It galled me to call myself stupid, but I knew it would feed his male ego. Sure enough, he sat up a little straighter, preening like a peacock.

"Anyway, I was supposed to meet her up north in Hilltop. She warned me I'd better show up alone. I—I just couldn't think of anything but protecting our family. I see now that I wasn't thinking straight. I got up there and waited at the little café she had mentioned, but she never showed up. I even found a room and went back to the café the next day. Nothing. Thank God you know everything now! I feel safe again, baby!" I nuzzled his lips, his cheek, his ear. Listening to his heavy breathing, I knew I had him.

"Jess—sugar—let's go upstairs." He kissed me back, frantically, fervently.

"What's wrong with right here, baby?" I moaned a little. "Oh, I've missed you so."

And that was that—hook, line, and sinker. Men are so predictable.

# CHAPTER SEVEN

The next morning was hectic. We all woke up a little late, and I rushed through doing the girls' hair. The two little ones squealed a bit when I pulled their braids tight, but Amelia didn't say a word. She usually fussed and told me she was old enough to do her own hair, but not today. Dan had an early appointment, so he left before I could cook him breakfast.

That's one of the things I pride myself on—cooking my family a hot breakfast every morning. Today the oatmeal didn't seem to want to thicken, so I just told the girls to eat it anyway. "It's just as healthy for you, thick or thin," I said, gathering their book bags. "Now let's get cracking—we don't want to be late for school." I bundled them all in the car and took off.

The school day went by in a blur. I ate lunch in my classroom, because I just wasn't in the mood for all the silly chatter I'd have to endure in the teachers' lunchroom. The children, thank goodness, were obedient and silent. They knew that I was in no mood for improper behavior.

Finally the day was done. I was walking out to the parking lot when a voice stopped me.

"Jess, Jess, do you have a minute?" It was Amelia's teacher, Kathy Barnes. Stifling the urge to cut her off, I smiled and said, "Why surely, Kathy. What's up? I don't have much time—I don't like the girls to wait by the car too long. You can't be too careful with your children, you know." Kathy couldn't have children and was trying to adopt. Normally I wouldn't have thrown in that last remark, but she was making me late.

"Well, that's just it, Jess," she said, getting red in the face. "It's the girls I want to talk with you about—well, really, Amelia."

I looked at her coolly. She stood there, sweaty and nervous, and I just waited her out. Finally, wringing her hands, she spoke.

"You know I just love Amelia—she's so smart, really my best reader. But something seems to be bothering her, and I think it's affecting her schoolwork."

I raised one eyebrow. "Yes?"

She became even more flustered. "Well, it's just, I don't know—is there anything at home that might be bothering her? Oh, I don't mean with you and Dan," she added hastily, seeing how I tightened my stance, "I just thought—I don't know—maybe a pet died, or maybe she's having problems with her sisters, or—"

"Kathy, thank you for being such a concerned teacher," I said, so syrupy sweet I almost sickened myself. "But honestly, there's not a thing wrong with Amelia that a little discipline can't cure. I wonder if your expectations are high enough for her? She's always been one to take the easy way out, and believe me, she knows how to put on the Poor Pitiful Pearl act." I smiled. "You do know what I mean by Poor Pitiful Pearl, don't you? She was a doll that—"

"Yes, I remember. I had a Chatty Cathy myself," she giggled. "My parents thought it was funny, you know, because my name is Kathy and I like to talk—always have."

Shuddering inwardly, I put my hand on her shoulder. "Kathy, you're a great teacher," I said earnestly, looking her straight in the eyes, "Believe me, I will check with Amelia and see if there's anything bothering her, but I'm pretty sure that it's just fifth-grade-itis." I smiled as she laughed at the lame joke.

"I'm so glad we chatted, Jess. I just admire you so much,

both as a teacher and a mother. Amelia is lucky to have a mama like you."

I smoothed my hair and shifted my tote bag to my other shoulder. "You are just the sweetest thing. But now, I really do need to go—tonight is our family game night, and I promised the girls we'd make cookies, so we have to scoot."

"Oh, I'm so sorry! I shouldn't have kept you! And here are the girls now. They've been waiting so patiently. Bye-bye. See you tomorrow, Amelia." She dashed off, skirt hem drooping, hair flyaway, shoes unshined. Really, some people took no pride in their appearance at all.

Amelia and I stood still for a moment, looking at each other. Her gaze didn't waver, and I felt myself getting angry. Slow down, I told myself. Stay in control. The little ones were chatting with each other about some new cartoon character.

"So, Amelia, it seems you've been having some interesting conversations with Ms. Barnes. Do you have anything you'd like to tell me?"

"No . . . ma'am." There was just the briefest pause before the "ma'am."

"We'll talk about this later. Right now, because of you, we're late. We were going to make cookies tonight, but now we won't have time." I opened the car door and pushed her in. Well, if she wasn't going to move on her own, somebody had to do it for her, didn't they? Amanda and Abigail climbed in behind her.

"You're a bad sister, Amelia. Now we can't have cookies," said Amanda.

"Yeah, bad," chimed in Abigail.

"Now girls, I'm sure Amelia feels very sorry for causing us to be late. Don't you, Amelia?"

But Amelia simply looked out the car window and didn't respond.

We were just sitting down to dinner—my famous lemon chicken—when the phone rang. Dan started to get up, but I raised my hand.

"You just stay put, mister. You've been on your feet all day. I'll get it." He gave me a grateful look as he went back to his meal. The girls were toying with their food, more rearranging it than eating it, so I spoke sharply as I got up.

"You girls had better eat up if you want chocolate cake for dessert." It didn't escape my notice that Abigail and Amanda got right to it, but Amelia just stared stubbornly at her plate. Stifling a sigh, I went into the kitchen to answer the phone.

"Hello. Hello? If this is a solicitor, we're on the do-not-call list. Who is this, please?"

Finally a whispery voice came through the line. "Baby, it's me, your mama. Why didn't you answer my letters?"

I sank down on one of the kitchen stools. My mind was racing. There hadn't been any notification that the call was coming from the prison, so that could only mean one thing—she was out.

"Where are you?" I asked, my voice hushed. The chatter of my family drifted through from the other room.

"I'm right here in your town, baby. I need help. I need a place to stay. You're surely not going to deny your own flesh and blood, are you?" Her voice took on a whiney tone.

"How did you find me?"

"Oh, there's ways to get information, even in prison." She chuckled. "Maybe I should say, especially in prison. You'd be amazed at what's available. So are you going to help me, or what?"

I closed my eyes and took a deep breath. "You listen here,

Mama. I'll help you, but you've gotta keep your mouth shut, you hear? You need me, so you better get used to doing things my way."

There was a gasp on the other end of the line. "Well now, missie, aren't you high and mighty? You might get away with that kind of behavior from some old poor white trash, but I am your mama, and you'd better not forget it."

"Oh, I haven't forgotten that, Mama, much as I've tried. Now listen," I said, speaking faster. Any longer on the phone and Dan might come out to see what was going on. "Give me a number where I can reach you. I've got to get Dan and the girls prepared for this. I'm working tomorrow, but I can pick you up before dinner. I'll call you by five o'clock tomorrow, so make sure you're by the phone."

A light titter came from my mother. "You silly thing, I've got a cell phone. I'm not as old-fashioned as you might think. I'll make sure the ringer is turned up loud and clear. Now, don't you go forgetting to call, 'cuz I might just show up on your doorstep—or maybe your mother-in-law's doorstep. That'd be even better."

"Mama," I broke in, "just sit tight until tomorrow evening. I'll be there for you. Haven't I always been? I've gotta go. Don't talk to anybody until I come get you."

I clicked off the phone and went back into the dining room. Dan and the girls were laughing at some silly joke—even Amelia was guffawing. I sat down and started chewing my cold chicken dinner.

"Who was that, honey? You were so long I was going to send out the rescue dogs."

"I'll tell you after dinner," I said, glancing meaningfully at the girls. Dan got my drift, because he just nodded his head.

"Hey, didn't I hear you mention chocolate cake? What do you say, girls? Don't we all deserve some chocolate cake?"

"Cake! Cake! Cake!" they started chanting, bouncing up and down in their seats.

"Honestly Dan, you certainly know how to get our daughters to forget their manners. I'll bring cake to people who can sit like little ladies."

Dan made a mock sad face. "Guess that leaves me out, then."

The girls roared with laughter, and even I cracked a smile. "Oh you," was all I could say as I went to cut the cake.

Much later, after the girls were bathed and in bed, after I'd told Dan about my great-aunt who needed a place to stay temporarily, after we'd exhausted the topic to death, I lay in bed with Dan snoring beside me. The story could work, I told myself. I couldn't say she was my mother—there would be way too much to explain. But saying she was a decrepit old relative who needed help, someone I'd lost touch with over the years, sounded plausible. I'd worry later about how I'd get rid of her once she was here. I couldn't, just couldn't, have her with us permanently. I shivered as a chill ran down my back and closed my eyes. I felt myself drifting off. Then the dream began.

# CHAPTER EIGHT

It always started the same. I was sitting on the couch, struggling to stay awake. Mama had said she wouldn't be late, but it was already past midnight. Nathan was usually a good baby, but tonight he'd been fussy. I was worried that he might be running a fever, but Mama had told me not to fret.

"He's a little man, Jess—he's strong. He'll be fine." She winked at me. " 'Course, men will never be as strong as us women. We just let them think they are." With a trail of perfume and a rustle of satin, she was gone. I knew she wasn't going out with Matt, my stepdad. He'd called earlier to say he had to work late, and Mama had torn into him on the phone.

"I swear, Matthew, you work more and more and bring home less and less. If I was the suspicious type, I might think you had a little bit of something on the side."

She listened a bit, then started up again. "Well, if you think I'm gonna sit around waiting for you, you've got another think coming. Let me know when you decide to be a man." Even in my room, I could hear the phone slam down. Before I knew it, Mama was in my door.

"Jess Bell, I need you to watch the baby tonight. Your daddy"—she always called Matt that, even though I knew he wasn't my daddy—"has decided work is more important than me, so I'm just gonna let him know where his priorities should be."

I could tell she was in a mood, so I just muttered "Yes'm."

That was usually the safest answer when Mama was on a roll. I didn't mind watching Nathan. He was a sweet baby, with a dimpled smile and a cute little gurgly laugh. But today he'd been whiney and crying insistently, as though he expected someone to fix whatever was bothering him. I felt like telling him that sometimes there was no remedy for what ailed him, but I knew he wouldn't understand.

Then Mama was gone. I was back on the couch with my algebra book. Math had never been my strong point, and I was really struggling with algebra. I couldn't seem to reconcile numbers and letters jumbling up together in one subject. Just as I was getting deep into the first problem, Nathan started crying.

I found myself in his room, looking down in the crib at his red face and tense body. I wasn't sure how I got there. I reached down and picked him up, rocking him in my arms.

"Hush now, baby, you're okay. Big sister is here for you. Are you hungry? Wet? What's wrong, little man?"

It didn't take too long to cover all the bases of what might be ailing the baby. His shrieks had muted into gulping little whimpers. My heart broke for him.

"Try and sleep, Nate-nate," I said, as I backed out of the room. "Sister's gotta finish her math."

After that everything was sort of hazy—a mishmash of groping my way through algebra problems, walking the floor with Nathan, dozing off, only to be shocked awake by his yells. Finally I burst out crying, too.

"Damn you, *Mom*," I hollered to the uncaring living room walls. "Where the hell are you?" Calling her Mom instead of Mama was a measure of my frustration. She preferred the latter. I liked the former. It was usually safer just to give in and call her Mama, but right now I didn't care what was safe.

I flung myself onto the couch and put my hands over my ears. There didn't seem to be anything I could do for Nathan, and I was so tired. Finally I dragged myself up and stumbled into his room again.

"Baby, what's wrong? What can I do for you? I'm so sorry you're sick. You've got a bad, bad mama to leave you when you're not feeling well." I leaned over his crib and looked at him, my tears dripping on his blanket.

What to do? What to do? If Nathan didn't get to sleep soon, I wouldn't get to sleep, and I had an algebra quiz first thing in the morning. Suddenly I remembered something.

"Don't you worry, Nate-nate," I whispered as I patted his head. "I know what will help you."

He actually stopped crying for a minute and looked at me like he understood, but then the screaming started again.

I ran into the kitchen and pulled out the whiskey bottle from the cupboard over the refrigerator. I'd seen Mama do this a dozen times—why hadn't I thought of it before? Just a little slug of whiskey in his bottle would put Nathan to sleep in no time. I grabbed one of his empty baby bottles and poured in an inch or two of alcohol, then filled the rest with apple juice. He loved apple juice.

Hurrying back into his room, I all but shoved the bottle into his mouth. At first he fussed and tried to push it away, but then he started sucking it down. Before too long his eyelids were drooping.

"Thank God," I muttered as I tiptoed out of the room. I settled back down on the couch and managed to finish all of my algebra before 1:30, which was just about the time Mama came waltzing in. By the smell of her, she'd had her own share of whiskey tonight. That was unusual, because she rarely drank any hard liquor. She said people who had to rely on alcohol to have fun were weaklings.

"Hey baby girl, how'd it go tonight? Everything okay?"

"Sure, Mama. I've got to get to bed. I have school tomor-row."

" 'Course you do, sweet thing. Mama's here now, I'll take care of everything. Uh, Jess-girl—"

She paused and looked confused. Maybe it was the liquor; I didn't know and I didn't care.

"What is it, Mama? I'm really tired."

"Did your daddy call while I was out?" Her eyes held a plead-ing look that was unusual for her.

"No, ma'am. G'night." I turned and headed into my room, but I clearly heard the crash of the table lamp hitting the floor. Oh well, that was her problem. I fell into bed and into a deep and dreamless sleep.

The next thing I know, Mama is shaking me awake, saying something about Nathan not breathing. My heart starts beating so fast I think it might jump out of my chest—and then I wake up. I mean, really wake up. I've had that same dream about the night Nathan died every few months since it happened. It's got-ten so I hardly know what's real anymore and what is the dream. The one thing that stays the same is the panicky feeling I wake up with. It always takes me a while to calm my breathing and feel somewhat normal. But once I wake up from the dream, I know there'll be no sleeping the rest of the night. I ease myself out of bed so I won't disturb Dan and go into the kitchen to sit at the table and work on some lesson plans. I'll think about Mama tomorrow.

One thing I know for sure—she'll be part of tomorrow, and who knows how many more to come.

# CHAPTER NINE

By the time Dan and the girls were up, I'd made blueberry pancakes, homemade syrup, and fresh-squeezed orange juice. I hadn't been able to go back to sleep after my rude awakening, so I decided to be productive. I'd also planned out just how I was going to handle this whole Mama mess. I shook my head and sighed. It was hard to believe that I was smack dab in the middle of her chaos again after all these years.

I was thinking so hard I jumped when Dan came into the kitchen.

"Whoa," he said, laughing. "Didn't mean to scare you."

I plastered a smile on my face. "You're not scary, you're sweet." I gave him a peck on the cheek. "Umm, sweetie, I think I'm going to ask Norma to watch my class for the last hour of school today. That way I can pick up M—I mean, Auntie Mae. Do you think you could get the girls on your way home from work? They can stay in the after-school program until you can get there."

"Sure. Mmm, do I smell blueberry pancakes? You are the best wife ever!" He hugged me from behind, and I forced myself not to stiffen. "I guess you want some alone time with your auntie before we all descend on her. How long has it been since you've seen her, again?"

"It's been at least—oh, I guess about twenty years. It was at my parents' funeral. She's my mama's older sister. She offered to have me live with her, but I was closer to my dad's side of the family, so I stayed with them. We just lost touch over the years."

"Well, I think it's great to finally have some contact with your family. It'll be good for the girls, too, to get to know more about your roots. Hey, it looks like that pancake is just about ready."

I flipped the pancake onto a plate with my spatula. "Ready when you are, kind sir." Just about then the girls came in and everything was rush-rush for a few minutes.

As my family sat eating contentedly, I sipped my coffee. Get to know my roots, my ass. I was going to make it my business for my girls to never know about the evil seed that spawned them.

"Mama, aren't you going to eat? Have a bite of mine." Little Abigail pushed her fork in my mouth.

"Thank you, darling," I sputtered as I gulped it down. "You are the sweetest thing."

"What about me, Mama? I'm sweet, too!" Amanda jumped out of her chair and ran to me, burying her sticky face in my skirt. I held back a shudder. She didn't know any better.

"Of course you are, baby. You're all Mama's sweet little girls." I glanced at Amelia as I stroked her sister's hair. She was studiously avoiding my look as she stared intently at her plate. What was wrong with that girl, anyway? Why didn't she appreciate having a perfect family, with loving parents? She just didn't care.

"Okay, time for school," I cried, bounding out of my chair. "Chop-chop, let's go. There's going to be a surprise waiting for you when you get home today!" I had managed to get Dan to agree not to tell the girls about "Aunt Mae" in advance. I told him I wanted them to meet her without any preconceived notions, but really I was just putting off the inevitable. A heavy weight settled in my chest when I thought about Mama meeting my innocent little children. She was tainted, evil, and I'd do whatever it took to protect my family from her.

Two o'clock finally came, and I scooted out to the parking lot. As soon as I got in the car, I pulled out my cell.

"Mama? I'll be by to get you in about ten minutes. Are you all packed and ready?"

"I sure am, darlin'. I swear, I'm just so excited to see your big old house and fancy things. You done good, sugar."

*No thanks to you,* I thought, but aloud I said, "Now remember, you're my Aunt Mae. You're my poor dead mama's older sister, and you've fallen on hard times, so we're taking you in—for a while."

"Whatever. Just get your butt over here. I'm ready to be shed of this place."

A few minutes later I pulled up in front of the shabby motel she'd directed me to. Funny, I'd lived in this town for fifteen years, and I never even knew this place existed. A shrill sound interrupted my musings.

"Yoo-hoo, yoo-hoo, sugar! Oh my gawd, I'm so glad to see you! I can't even tell you." Mama threw her bag into the back-seat and jumped into the car. "Let's go—step on it. I'm so done with this kind of trash."

"What's the big hurry, Mama?" I eased my foot onto the gas. I didn't want to peal out and get dirt all over my nice clean car. "Anybody'd think you were trying to run out on a bill or some—oh, no, Mama!" I slammed my fist on the steering wheel. "Don't tell me you're up to your old tricks!"

"I do not know to what you are referring," she said, all snooty. "Just let's get the hell out of here."

As I slowly pulled out onto the highway, I could see someone running out of the motel office. He was a big man, with a red face, and I could just imagine what he was yelling. He was waving a paper in one hand.

"Don't worry, darlin', he won't be able to get your license plate. He can't see a thing without his glasses, and he's too vain to wear 'em." She giggled girlishly. "Oh, we are going to have such *fun,* just like the old days. And I can't wait to meet your hunky hubby and your cute little girls—are there two, or three? You didn't keep me very well informed while I was away."

I kept my eyes straight ahead as I answered her. "There are three, and we'd better get a few things straight. Dan doesn't have a clue about you or where you've been. He thinks we're doing the Christian thing by taking in an elderly relative in need." I glanced over when I said this and saw her face screw up in distaste. "I expect you to behave yourself and not cause any trouble. As soon as I can get enough money together for you to make a fresh start somewhere, you'll be leaving town. And Mama, there's one more thing."

"Yes?" she said snappishly.

"Dan's insurance policy is tied up in a trust fund. If he dies, there's nobody going to get any cash except the girls."

She opened her eyes wide. "I'm sure I don't know why that would be of any interest to me."

I really looked at her for the first time. It was obvious she had freshly dyed her hair—it had a sort of metallic glow to it. She was wearing too much makeup and a tight T-shirt paired with a denim miniskirt. I was going to have to give her a makeover before Dan and the girls got home. I sighed and turned toward the mall.

"C'mon, Mama, we're going shopping."

She squealed and clapped her hands. "What did I say? Just like the old days."

# CHAPTER TEN

I looked critically at Mama as she sat in the salon chair, a sullen look on her face. A shiver ran down my spine. With that expression on her face, she looked so much like Amelia. I gave myself a shake and spoke to the stylist.

"That's just perfect. Thank you so much."

"Perfect for an old biddy," muttered Mama, reaching up to touch her ashy blond locks.

"Now, Auntie, you *are* a blonde. That's not such an old lady color."

She snorted. "You call this blond? I call it gray. And it's so short now."

I winked at the stylist, who was beginning to look anxious. "It's just perfect," I said again more firmly. "My aunt will grow to love it, I'm sure."

As we left the salon and walked to the car, Mama's mood did not improve. "I swear," she whined, "between this fuddy-duddy hairdo and the boring clothes we bought, I'll hardly recognize myself in the mirror."

I stopped in the middle of the parking lot. "Clothes *we* bought? You better keep things straight. *I* bought the clothes, *I* paid for your hair style, and *I'm* the one who is giving you a place to live rent-free. For all of that, I'm only asking you to behave yourself and remember that you're my dear sweet Auntie Mae. Don't worry, it won't be for long. I'm sure you're not going to enjoy this any more than I will. I just need some time to get a little money together and settle you in your own place—preferably on the other side of the country."

Mama's eyes filled with tears. "Do you really hate me that much? We were so close when you were little—more like sisters than mother and daughter. Why are you being so cruel?"

I walked to the car and threw open the passenger door. "Get in." My voice was calm. Steady.

Mama looked at me and smiled, her tears dried as fast as she had shed them. "No problem, sugar. But maybe you'd best realize that it's not all about you helping me. I have a few tricks up my sleeve, you know. And I'm not afraid to use 'em." She plopped down on the car seat and fastened her seat belt, humming a little tune.

I got in the car and started toward home. I didn't look at Mama and she didn't look at me. My mind was racing. Just what did she mean by those comments? Sure, she could tell Dan the whole sordid truth about actually being my mother, but I could handle that. I'd just tell him she was senile, deranged. No, she had something else in mind. But what? She was the murderess, not me. She was the ex-con.

I sneaked a glance at her. She still had that smile on her face. Why hadn't she just died in prison? It would have made things so much easier. Now I was going to have to be on guard every minute of every day. I knew my mama—she would stop at nothing to get what she wanted.

We pulled up to the house. Mama's eyes opened wide as she took in the spacious lawn, Tudor-style house, and beautiful rose beds.

"My, oh my," she breathed. "This is a house fit for a queen. Think it's big enough for the two of us?" She looked at me slyly.

I didn't respond. I have too much dignity to be taken in by

such tricks. I calmly walked to the back of the car and took out her bag.

"Come on in. I'll show you to your room." She followed me, stopping to exclaim over the cobbled walkway and the scent of the roses.

We have a very nice guest room, with its own bath. I had decorated it in a Victorian style, with lots of floral prints. Mama went into raptures when she saw it.

"Sugar, this is just beautiful! Did you pick out these colors and fabrics? I just bet you did—you always had an eye for prettiness." She hugged me tight. I found myself hugging her back.

I stepped back abruptly. "I'm glad you like it." I prided myself on not letting my voice shake. "But keep in mind, this is only temporary."

She nodded and began to unpack. As she did so, I heard Dan's car pull up into the drive. I grabbed Mama's arm.

"They're here! Now remember who you are—my dear old Aunt Mae. And be on your best behavior. Dan thinks I came from a refined family."

She shook off my grip. "I hardly need my child to tell me how to act," she said, her voice dripping icicles. "I'm the one who taught you your manners, missy."

The front door slammed open. I winced as I heard it strike the wall. I had reminded Dan not to do that at least one hundred times. Excited voices bubbled from the entry.

"Mama, Mama, we're home!"

"Honey, where are you?"

I smoothed my dress and walked out to meet them, Mama close behind.

"Here we are—just getting Aunt Mae settled in her room."

Dan approached Mama with his hand outstretched. "It's so good to finally meet some of Jess's family. I hope you'll be comfortable here."

Almost before he stopped speaking, Mama reached out and embraced him.

"Oh, Dan, thank you so much for taking me in! Why, you are even more handsome than Jess said! And these must be your precious girls! Now, let me guess who's who."

She put one finger on her cheek as though she were deep in thought. Dan and the girls stared at her, entranced.

"I've got it!" she exclaimed. "You must be Abigail," she continued, hugging my littlest. "And you are Amanda," followed by more hugs. "And this—this can only be Amelia."

Instead of hugging Amelia, Mama stood back as though she were admiring a princess. Amelia smiled shyly at her. My stomach twisted in knots. When was the last time she had smiled at me?

"Oh, Amelia, I would have known you anywhere! You look just like your mama did when she was your age! Oh, my goodness"—her voice choked with tears—"it is so wonderful to finally meet you!"

To my shock, Amelia stepped toward my mother and took her hand. "I'm so glad to meet you, too, Auntie. I'm really glad you're here."

As Mama and Amelia clasped hands, I struggled to calm my breathing and remain in control. This was bad, very bad. I should have anticipated that the two of them would forge a bond. They were two of a kind.

# CHAPTER ELEVEN

The night went fairly smoothly. I made a roast with mashed potatoes and gravy. Mama oohed and aahed over the meal. "Do you remember Sunday meals at home, dear heart? We *always* had roast on Sundays."

It was all I could do not to roll my eyes. Mama apparently remembered things differently than I did. I recalled Sunday dinners of frozen pizza and soda. I glanced at Dan and saw a puzzled expression on his face.

"I thought you lived with relatives on your dad's side of the family, Jess. Did you get together for extended family meals often?"

Before I could answer, Mama chimed in. "Oh yes, Dan, we were all so close. Why, we'd get together at the drop of a hat. Both sides of the family got along so well. Jess's parents were simply lovely people, and they enjoyed nothing more than hosting family get-togethers. Those are such happy memories." She dabbed at her eyes with her napkin.

I had to hand it to her—she was a pro. She knew just how to turn a sticky situation to her favor. I kept my head down and concentrated on cutting my meat.

Then Amelia piped up. "Auntie Mae, what was Mommy like when she was little?"

I froze as I waited for the response.

"Oh, my dear, she was the sweetest little thing. Pretty as a picture—just like you—and so talented. She could play the piano like a virtuoso, and she danced like a fairy—light as a feather. And of course she was always on the honor roll at school. I swear, she was just the perfect child." She smiled benignly at me.

I could only sit with my mouth open. I had wanted to take piano and dance lessons as a child—in fact, I'd begged for the opportunity. Mama always said she was going to sign me up, but it never happened. Amelia was looking at me with interest.

"How come you never play piano now, Mommy?"

"That's right, Jess. I'd love to hear you play. We have the baby grand, but I've never seen you touch it." Dan put down his fork and leaned toward me with curiosity on his face.

"Oh, I sort of lost the desire after my parents died. It just—it just didn't seem important anymore."

Mama reached over and took my hand across the table. "Now Jess, you shouldn't let such talent go. Why, I bet that if you sat down at the piano right now, it would all come back to you."

I pulled my hand away. "Maybe, but right now it's time for dessert. Who wants brownies with ice cream?"

As the little ones squealed in delight, I got up from the table and headed into the kitchen. Damn Mama anyhow! What was she playing at? I could no more play the piano than a monkey could write Shakespeare.

Soon enough dinner was over and the kids were finally in bed. Dan had volunteered to oversee baths and bedtime stories so "Auntie Mae" and I could have time to visit.

"What on earth are you thinking? What was all that about me being a pianist? You know I never took lessons!" I hissed the words but she could hear me clearly enough.

She batted her eyes at me. "Now, Jess, I have no doubt that you could do anything you set your mind to. If you want to be an accomplished musician, you can be. Maybe you should start taking lessons now. It's never too late, you know." She sipped her after-dinner coffee.

"Whatever." I plopped down in the chair next to her. "Just remember, we're supposed to be long-lost relatives. You shouldn't know much about me—not that you ever did."

She winced at the harsh words. "Sugar, you know I would never have left you if I'd had any choice. That dad-blamed DA was out to get me. I love you, Jess Bell—I always have." She had a pleading look on her face,

"Sorry, Mama—I mean, Aunt Mae. I don't have time to hash over the past. I've got to get up early tomorrow."

"Whatever for? Tomorrow's Saturday, isn't it? I thought we might take the girls to the mall, or maybe a movie, or—"

"No way." I cut her off. "Amelia has math tutoring at ten, and Amanda and Abigail have tumbling class at eleven. Then they all have bell-ringing practice at the church at two. This is what *real* mothers do, Ma—Aunt Mae. They make sure their children are involved in wholesome, uplifting activities. They don't spend their time going out carousing, leaving their children to fend for themselves." I could feel my face flushing as my breathing intensified.

It was as though a shutter closed over Mama's eyes. "I understand. You're the perfect mother—I see that." She got up and moved toward the hall. "Is it all right with you if I tell the girls good night? You wouldn't object to that, would you?"

"No," I mumbled. "Go ahead." Dan came into the room just as I finished speaking.

"Hey, Aunt Mae, the girls would like to give you good-night kisses." He looked so big and happy that I just couldn't stand it. I looked away.

"Can you believe it? That's just what I was about to do!" Mama glided out of the room. A few minutes later I heard giggles and squeals coming from the two little ones' room. They were still young enough to be scared of the dark, and it seemed to help for them to share a room.

I kept listening as Dan sat down beside me and opened the newspaper. I strained my ears to hear what was happening in Amelia's room. I could detect a low buzz of voices, nothing more.

"Honey, what's the matter? You're so tense. Want a neck rub?"

I pulled away from my husband. "No, that's okay. I'm just tired. It's been a busy day."

"That's for sure. I've got to tell you, Aunt Mae has been a pleasant surprise. I wasn't sure quite what to expect, but she is so full of life. You'd never think she'd been down and out." He shook his head admiringly.

I got up abruptly. "I'm going to say good night to the girls. They've had a busy day, too."

Dan was already immersed in his paper. "Uh-huh."

I walked stealthily down the hall to Amelia's room. The floor creaked just as I got to her door.

"Why, here you are, sugar. I was just telling Amelia that I'd take her to her tutoring tomorrow. You need a little time to yourself. After all, you and Dan are doing so much for me, I want to contribute in some way." Mama was sitting on Amelia's bed with her arm around her. My heart twisted. Amelia never let me hug her anymore.

"That sounds great, Auntie, except you don't have a car. How are you planning on getting her to tutoring?" My voice sounded much calmer than I felt.

"We're going to ride bikes, Mommy!" Amelia fairly bounced up and down in excitement. "Did you know Auntie Mae can ride a bike? Did you?"

"I guess I forgot," I said woodenly. "We'll talk about this tomorrow. Go to bed now. Sweet dreams."

Amelia snuggled down into her pillows. I turned to look at

Mama as she left the room. She was humming a tune and doing a dance step down the hall. This could only mean trouble.

# Chapter Twelve

My eyes snapped open at five o'clock the next morning. I felt on high alert. It took me a minute to remember why. Oh, right—Mama. Mama was back, ready to destroy the life I had built so carefully. She was a like a loose cannon, barreling down the battlefield, annihilating everything in sight.

I looked over at Dan and sighed. He was sleeping so peacefully, snoring gently as he lay sprawled out on his back. I had tried to get him to sleep on his side, but he wouldn't. I'd told him that it would help him breathe more easily, but he just smiled and said, "Whatever, honey." Maybe if he had to listen to the noise, he'd take it more seriously.

I sat up and shoved my feet into my slippers. No one seemed to understand how much I did to keep things running smoothly in our home. For example, I had to get up by five in order to have time for thirty minutes on the treadmill. Keeping physically fit is an important part of being a good wife and mother. Then I'd have time to do a load of laundry or weed the garden (depending on the day of the week), and jump into the shower and get ready for the day. I'd start breakfast before Dan and the kids got up, because I knew they loved waking up to the smell of a hot breakfast cooking.

I made my way into the family room and the treadmill. Just as I was crossing the hall, Mama popped out of her room.

"Mama! You scared me half to death! What are you doing up so early?"

"To tell you the truth, sugar, I got into the habit of early rising when I was—you know."

"Locked up?" My voice sounded harsh, even to me.

Mama just looked at me steadfastly. "Yes, that's right. When I was illegally incarcerated." She came closer and peered intently into my face. "You remember that, don't you? How I was unjustly accused? How I took responsibility for actions that were not my own?"

I stepped back. "I don't know what you're talking about. I have to get on with my day! I have to start my routine!"

I must have sounded a little frantic, because Mama patted my hand and crooned, "There, there, dear one. Don't you fret. Can I help you with anything?"

"No—no. I've got everything under control. I can handle it."

"Well, why don't I just get the coffee started and read the paper. You do what you need to do." She turned toward the kitchen.

I watched her as she sashayed down the hall. How could she be so—nonchalant? Was it possible she didn't remember our shared past? I shook my head and snorted. More likely she just remembered things in her own revisionist history.

An hour later, Mama had finished the paper and I was dressed for the day. I crept into Amanda and Abigail's room.

"Good morning, good girls. Are you ready for a perfectly beautiful day?" I bent down and kissed them both.

"Mama! Mama! We love you!" They both reached up their little hands to my face.

Amanda sat up and looked around. "Where's Auntie Mae? She didn't leave, did she?" She looked ready to cry.

Abigail popped up like a little clone of her sister. "I want Auntie Mae!" she insisted, her lower lip trembling.

I stood back, taken by surprise. "Why girls, she's still here. There's nothing to be upset about. And besides, you've got me.

Mama's here, now and forever." I held out my arms to them.

They both snuggled in to me. The heat of their little bodies warmed my heart. As I was relaxing and enjoying the moment, I suddenly pulled back. I could hear a low murmur of voices from Amelia's room.

"Come on now, itty-bitties. Time to get up and brush away the sleepy-ticks." The girls giggled as I stepped out of their room into the hall. I walked very deliberately toward Amelia's room, being sure not to step on the squeaky board.

"And your mama was just the sweetest thing," Mama was saying. "She and I used to love to go shopping together."

"But Auntie Mae, I thought you didn't spend that much time with Mama when she was little." Amelia's high little voice piped out the door.

"Well you see sugar, there's a little secret about your mama and me. She—"

I strode briskly into the room. "Good morning, ladies. Ready for a lovely day? Amelia, would you rather have pancakes or waffles this morning?"

Amelia sank back on her pillows with a sullen look on her face. "I don't care."

"Well, I just dearly love waffles!" cried Mama, jumping up briskly. "What can I do to help?"

I was about to decline her assistance when I realized something. If I left her here with Amelia, who knew what mischief the two of them might get up to?

"As a matter of fact, *Aunt Mae,*" I said, emphasizing the title, "I could use some help. Would you mind terribly juicing some oranges for me?"

"I'd love to! Want to help Auntie with the juice, sweetie?" She smiled at Amelia.

Before Amelia could answer, I broke in. "Maybe she can in a bit, but Amelia needs to get ready for the day first. Hip-hop, jump in the shower, and don't forget to make your bed."

Amelia nodded without speaking and slid out of bed. Mama and I walked to the kitchen.

"Now Mama, maybe you want to tell me just what you and Amelia were talking about this morning?" I had my back to her as I stirred the waffle batter.

She bustled around putting the oranges into a bowl and getting another for the peels. "Oh, just chatting. A little grandmother to granddaughter—oops, I mean aunt to niece chitchat." She put her hand over her mouth in an exaggerated gesture of embarrassment at her slip of the tongue.

However, I knew it was no slip. Mama was a threat—to me and to my family. She couldn't be trusted now any more than she could be back when I was a child. I beat the batter a little harder. Well, Mama, the difference was, I was no longer a child. I could take care of things myself.

# Chapter Thirteen

My mind was clicking along at a furious pace during breakfast. I was thinking so hard that Dan had to ask me twice to get him some more coffee. He is so lucky to have a wife like me who enjoys serving her family.

It was while I was in the kitchen pouring his second cup that it came to me. I was so excited I even laughed a little out loud. Mama thought she could outsmart me, but there was no way that would happen.

"Hey, Aunt Mae, I forgot to tell you about my surprise for you," I said casually as I sat back down at the table.

"A surprise? Oh, I just love surprises! What is it? No, don't tell me—let me guess." She put one finger alongside her mouth. "Help me out, girls—what do you think my surprise is?"

"A puppy!" squealed Amanda. Abigail clapped her hands in glee and chanted, "A puppy! A puppy!"

"Don't be dumb," sneered Amelia. "You know Mama doesn't like animals."

"It's not that I don't like them, it's just that they're—"

"Messy," muttered Amelia, bowing her head and letting her hair cover her face.

"Okay, so not a puppy or a kitten," said Mama, jumping into the uncomfortable moment. "Maybe a chocolate cake? You're such a good baker, Jess-girl."

"Better than chocolate, Aunt Mae. How would you like a day at the spa? Manicure, pedicure, and a facial—my treat."

Mama jumped up from her chair and leaned over the table to hug me. "You are such a dear! Every woman loves being pampered. Will you be with me?"

I shook my head. "Sorry, I can't reschedule all the girls' activities today. I'll barely have time to get you to the salon by ten thirty after we take Amelia to tutoring. You should just about be done with your day when the girls are finished with bell-ringing practice at the church. Maybe we'll do it together another time."

Amelia looked up at Mama. "But we were going to ride bikes together. You were going to take me to tutoring." Her blue eyes glistened with the tears she would not allow herself to shed. I knew the feeling; I'd had plenty of disappointments from Mama in my day.

"Oh sugar, we'll do it next week for sure. I can't say no to your mama when she's planned such a fabulous day for me, now can I?"

I smiled as Amelia shook her head slowly. But then she turned a look on me of such—I guess the only word is hatred—that it took my breath away. I rose from the table.

"Dan, sweetie, could you do me the biggest favor? Could you stack the dishes in the dishwasher for me? I've got to make a few quick calls before we get going on the day."

Dan also stood up and gave me a quick hug. "Of course I can. And maybe three little munchkins would like to help me." He smiled at the girls. "You make your calls, and Aunt Mae, you get ready for your day of beauty—not that you need it."

Mama laughed prettily. "Get along with you, you sweet talker. I hope Jessie knows how lucky she is to have a man like you."

"I do, I certainly do. Thanks, honey," I said, giving him a quick peck on the cheek. "Help your daddy, girls."

I hurried to my bedroom and shut the door. Grabbing my cell, I dialed the salon. "Jacques? It's Jessie. I need the biggest favor from you." A few minutes later, I clicked the phone off with a sigh of relief. It would mean an extra-big tip, but they would fit Mama in today. I fished the secret credit card out from the lingerie drawer. That little piece of plastic was really coming through for me—first it financed my getaway, and now it was delivering Mama away from private time with my daughter. I'd just have to remember to get to the bill before Dan did.

I sat down on the bed and took a deep breath. Things were moving fast, and I needed a plan. Right now I felt as though I was just keeping one step ahead of Mama, and that wasn't good enough. I'd have to make some time soon to sit quietly and figure out my next move—no, my next *series* of moves.

I stretched my shoulders as I waited in the car for the girls to be through with practice. It had been a hectic day, but it was worth all the trouble. Mama was safely isolated at the salon and I'd managed to get everyone to all of their activities on time. Now I finally had a minute to myself to plan.

The car was warm and I felt my eyelids droop. My head nodded. Maybe I could allow myself just a minute or two—just a minute . . .

*"Mama, Mama," I called as I ran through the house. Was it the house in Needles or the one in Sacramento? Or maybe the old scary house in Mississippi? It seemed to be a combination of all of them. "Where are you? I'm scared."*

*Suddenly Mama appeared in front of me. Her hair was flame red, but her green eyes shot even brighter sparks as she glared at me.*

*"What have you done, child? What have you done? Do you expect me to clean up all your messes? Well, do you?" Her voice roared like thunder.*

*"No, Mama. I'm sorry, I'm so sorry. Please don't be mad at me."*

*I cowered in front of her like a mewling little baby.*

*She abruptly changed from an angry virago to a sweet and gentle mother. "Don't you worry, Jess-girl. I'll protect you, I'll save you. I'm your mother and I'll never let anyone hurt you. Come to Mama. I'll never let you go."*

I woke with a start, my face sweaty and my heart beating a mile a minute. It hadn't been like that—had it? No, she had never shown me such gentleness and love—had she?

"Mama, Mama, we were the bestest ones today! We can ring real good!" Amanda and Abigail ran up to the car and piled in. Amelia trailed behind as usual.

"I'm sure you can, sweeties. How about you, Amelia? Did you have a good practice?"

"I guess," she muttered, getting into the car and slamming the door.

"Okay, girls, it's time to pick up Auntie Mae. Do you think she'll be transformed into a fairy princess?" I kept my tone light.

"She's already beautiful, Mommy. She's sooo pretty." Abigail rolled her eyes dramatically.

I glanced back in the rearview mirror and saw Amelia's look of disgust. I gave myself a silent congratulations for reaching one stage of my plan. I'd succeeded in showing Amelia that "Auntie Mae" was nothing more than a self-centered, shallow fraud. She couldn't really care for anyone but herself.

Could she?

# CHAPTER FOURTEEN

Mama was ecstatic over her "day of beauty," as she insisted on calling it. The girls—even Amelia—had exclaimed over her shocking-pink nail color and immediately began begging to have their nails painted in a matching shade.

"Now girls, you know how I feel about that," I said firmly. "Clear polish is more appropriate for children, with maybe a pale blush pink for special occasions." Out of the corner of my eye I saw Mama and Amelia share a smirk. It hadn't taken long for Amelia to forgive her grandma—I mean, Aunt Mae.

Mama surprised me that night by announcing that she wanted to make a special dinner—"to thank you for such a wonderful treat," she said. She had cooked minimally when I was a child, and it wasn't anything she really enjoyed. In fact, I had taken over most of the kitchen duty by the time I was eight years old.

She insisted that Dan and I both relax in the living room with a glass of wine and swept into the kitchen with the girls following her. "I'll need some helpers for this meal," she had said, and all three girls were excited at the opportunity to cook. I preferred to work solo in the kitchen, myself. The children had a tendency to spill things and make a mess. I wondered cynically who would be cleaning up after this gourmet delight.

Dinner was amazingly good. Mama had outdone herself, starting with a salad that had interesting ingredients and following with meatloaf and mashed potatoes. Dessert was chocolate mousse. Dan was effusive in his praise.

"This is great, Aunt Mae," he gushed. "I don't know when I've had better meatloaf—except for yours, of course, honey," he added, giving me a conciliatory smile.

I smiled back. "It really is good, Auntie, but I'm more impressed with the salad. It has such a good flavor, and lots of crunchy ingredients. I'll have to get the recipe from you."

Mama laughed prettily. "Oh no, I never give away my cooking secrets. Besides, Amelia did most of the work on the salad. She's got a real talent for the culinary arts."

I looked at Amelia in surprise. She had never acted interested in cooking before. As usual lately, her head was down, half-hidden by her hair.

"Honey, you did a great job. Maybe you'd like to help me in the kitchen sometime."

"Maybe," she mumbled.

The rest of the evening passed peacefully enough. Dan shocked me by insisting on doing the dishes. He would sometimes help clean up if I asked him, but he'd never volunteered before. What kind of web was Mama spinning? My whole family seemed to be caught in it.

About three o'clock in the morning I was awakened suddenly by a stabbing pain in my stomach. I was wet with sweat.

"Dan—Dan," I tried to say, but my tongue felt swollen. I could only get out an incomprehensible mewl. Dan snorted briefly and then rolled over. I couldn't expect any help from him.

I slid onto the floor. The pain was so intense that I couldn't stand. Instead, I crawled to the bathroom. The cool tile felt heavenly as I sprawled out on it, clutching my stomach. Then the rolling bouts of nausea started. I barely made it to the toilet in time to empty my gut, heaving again and again until I slumped over the white porcelain, completely exhausted.

"Honey, what's wrong?" Dan was suddenly standing behind me, his voice worried. My retching must have finally broken through his sweet repose.

"S-sick," I managed to say breathily. "Dinner."

"What? Dinner? You must be a little delirious. I bet you have that flu I've been reading about. You poor girl—here, let me help you up."

I slumped into his arms as he wiped my face tenderly with a damp washcloth. He was a good man, kind and caring. But why was he so stupid? Couldn't he see what was happening? Even in my exhausted state, I knew Mama was behind this.

Dan tried to get me to go back to bed, but I resisted. I spread-eagled on the floor, savoring the coldness against my sweat-soaked body. He finally gave up and covered me with a thin blanket.

"Should I call nine-one-one? Are you going to be okay?" He was actually wringing his hands.

I waved him away weakly. "I'm okay," I whispered. "Go back to bed."

"No, I'm up now. I'll go and get you some water. You must be completely dehydrated." He walked out of the bedroom.

I curled up in a fetal position, still clutching my stomach. I must have dozed off, because the next thing I knew Dan was back, bringing a glass of water to my lips.

"Here, drink this. You've got to replace the fluids you lost. Any better? Think you could get back in bed?"

I drank and nodded, letting him guide me back to bed. I collapsed onto it, and within minutes I was asleep. I know I must have dreamed—I always do—but when I next opened my eyes, I could only remember blackness.

"Dan!" I gasped, seeing the time on the bedside clock. "School—I have to—"

"It's okay, I called in for you," he said, walking out of the bathroom with his toothbrush in his hand. "Thank God Aunt Mae is here. She's getting the girls ready, and I'll drop them off at school on my way to work. If she weren't here to take care of you today, I'd stay home myself, but I have two oral surgeries scheduled. She's a real lifesaver."

I slumped back against my pillows. I knew it was useless to protest. He was convinced that Mama was an angel of mercy. Just like all the other men in her life, he couldn't see the evil that lurked inside her.

He leaned down and kissed me lightly on the forehead. "Just rest. You had a rough night."

I nodded, not trusting myself to speak. He grabbed his jacket and walked out of the bedroom, softly shutting the door.

My stomach felt better than it had earlier, but I'd developed a throbbing headache right behind my left eye. Ignoring it as best I could, I gritted my teeth and got out of bed. I grabbed the chair from my dressing table and wedged it under the doorknob. At least I'd have some warning if Mama tried to come in. I fell back in bed and slept.

# CHAPTER FIFTEEN

I slept off and on all day, just getting up a few times to refill the glass of water from the bathroom faucet. Once I heard the doorknob rattle and Mama saying something, but I just turned over and went back to sleep.

About three o'clock I finally felt as though I could get up and take a shower. I staggered to the bathroom, still weak from my illness and lack of food. The warm water felt good washing over me.

After I was dressed, I sat on the end of the bed and thought. This was a very unexpected development. Why would Mama want to hurt me? I was the one responsible for giving her a home to live in. There had to be some sort of motive, some payoff for her. There always was.

Then it came to me. Of course! I was a threat to her because I knew who she really was. If I was out of the picture, she could take over my whole family—my whole life. Dan would need someone to help with the house and the kids, and she'd be there, ready to step right in.

I stood up, full of resolve. I would never let that happen. I would never let that she-devil influence and raise my children. It was bad enough that I had lived through a childhood of hell—it would never happen to them.

I moved the chair away from the door and silently stepped out into the hall. I couldn't hear Mama anywhere. Tiptoeing toward the top of the staircase, I paused again. Not a sound. I hurried down the stairs and went into the kitchen.

The trash can under the sink was empty. Damn! Of course she would have thought of that. I looked more closely. Were those crushed leaves in the bottom of the bin? I shook them out onto a paper towel, examining them. They looked like wisteria leaves. I froze. We had wisteria growing on the side of the house. I had always warned the girls about touching the plants, especially the seed pods, because they were highly toxic. I knew this because Mama told me the same thing when I was a girl and we were visiting in Mississippi. I plopped down into one of the kitchen chairs, feeling dizzy.

Hadn't Mama said that Amelia had made the salad, the one with the crunchy ingredients? I shook my head to clear it. No, it couldn't have been Amelia. This was just another one of Mama's tricks, trying to get me to doubt my own daughter. And Mama would have known to just give me enough to make me sick, not kill me. She didn't want me to die—not yet, anyway. Of course, I had no real proof. A few crushed leaves in the garbage wouldn't convince anyone.

I was munching on some soda crackers when I heard the car pull up and the excited chatter of the girls as they tumbled out and came into the house.

"Auntie Mae, guess what? My teacher said I'm a superstar reader!" That was little Amanda's voice.

"Why, of course you are, sweet thing. Your mother was always the brightest in her class. I remember this one teacher she had—"

I met them at the door just in time to stop Mama's reminiscing. "Hello, babies! I'm so glad to see you all! I missed you this morning!"

Amanda and Abigail ran up and embraced me, but as usual Amelia held back. She finally came up and gave me a weak hug.

"I'm glad you feel better," she muttered as she slipped behind me and went into the house.

Both Mama and Dan were concerned to see me out of bed. They ushered me into the living room and forced me down onto the couch.

"Now, let's see," mused Mama, clasping her hands under her chin. "I'll make something light for dinner tonight—maybe soup?"

"No!" I almost shouted. "I don't want anything. Besides, it's not your job to cook. Dan can get takeout—right, honey?"

Dan stood in front of me, looking puzzled. "Well sure, honey, but I thought you didn't like the kids to eat fast food on school nights. And is that what you should be eating after you've been so sick?"

I briefly closed my eyes and then looked up at him, trying to compose my face and voice. God, he was so stupid sometimes!

"I didn't mean fast food, Dan. You can pick something up from Martello's Deli. In fact, I'll call it in. They make a great chicken soup and you love their roast beef sandwiches, don't you?"

A dreamy look came on his face. "Yeah, I do. Sounds great, sweetie. I'm just going to go change and then I'll be ready to go."

As he left the room, Mama remained, standing right in front of me. She had her arms crossed over her chest and stared accusingly at me.

"You don't trust me," she said in a trembling voice. "You think I did something to you. I would never—never—" Her voice broke and she sank into the armchair opposite me, burying her face in her hands.

I sighed loudly. I was too tired to deal with her nonsense.

"Oh, I trust you all right—I trust you not to change overnight. You're the same person you've always been. The difference is that now I'm an adult, not a helpless child. I can and will guard my family from your evilness."

She raised her head. "Helpless!" she spat out viciously. "You were far from helpless. You act like I never did anything to protect you. I just gave up my life to save yours, that's all! I lived in that miserable stinking prison while you enjoyed your freedom. Don't tell me—"

"No, *you* don't tell *me*! Don't act like you can tell me what to do, because you can't! *I'm* the one in charge now, and—"

I jumped up from the couch and leaped toward the stairs. Mama shrank back like she thought I was going to attack her— the silly bitch. No, there was something more important than fighting with her. We'd been overheard.

Sure enough, I was just in time to see Amelia run into her room and slam the door.

"Amelia!" I shouted hoarsely. "Amelia! Come down here!"

Instead, Dan came down the stairs. "What's wrong, Jess? Do you want me to talk with her? Is she acting up?"

I fell into his arms. "No, sweetie. It's nothing. I probably overreacted. Go on to the deli. I'll phone the order in right now and it should be ready when you get there."

He patted me on the head and went out the door. I picked up the phone and gave my order mechanically. Mama had taken the opportunity of Dan's interruption to slip away.

Sitting alone on the living room couch, I looked up at Amelia's closed door. It seemed to symbolize the lack of communication between my daughter and myself. How much had she heard? And more to the point, who would she tell?

# CHAPTER SIXTEEN

Amelia didn't come out of her room until Dan came home with the food. She didn't look at me or Mama, just sat at the table as usual with her hair covering her face. I chattered mindlessly about some TV show and other nonsense, trying to keep the focus off my miserable daughter. Mama was more subdued, responding to my conversational forays with as few words as possible.

Just as I was about to breathe a sigh of relief, Dan spoke up. I'd underestimated his level of parental concern.

"What's wrong, Amelia? Don't you feel well? You've hardly eaten a thing. Maybe you caught Mommy's flu bug." He patted her hand gently.

"I'm okay," she mumbled. "Just tired. Can I be excused?"

"*May* I be excused," I said automatically, then caught myself and looked at her. She was staring at me with the oddest expression—almost as though she didn't know who I was. The look sent shivers down my spine.

"Maybe an early bedtime will be good for you, sweetie. I'll be up in a minute to tell you good night." I stood up and put my arm around her shoulders. They were tensed up as though she were getting ready to flee. I dropped my arm to my side. "Take your plate out to the kitchen first, and don't forget to brush your teeth."

She jumped up and rushed out to the kitchen, then made her way upstairs. I sat back down and smiled brightly at Mama,

Dan, and the girls.

"That Amelia! She's turning into a teenager early, I guess. So moody." I turned to Abigail and Amanda. "Promise me you two won't ever grow up. I love you both just the way you are."

Simultaneously both little faces screwed up in unhappiness. Amanda even had tears in her eyes.

"We have to grow up, Mommy. Won't you still love us then?" Abigail's voice was pleading.

"Of course she will, cutie-pies! Mommy was just being silly, weren't you, Mommy?" Dan shot me a look that meant I'd better make this right. Mama just sat back in her chair, watching.

I got up and hugged both girls. "I love you a bushel and a peck, forever and ever. If you hurry and clear the table, you'll just have time for your favorite show. But remember, it's bedtime as soon as it's over."

They hugged me back and scampered off. I glanced at Dan and Mama. He had relaxed and looked content. Mama was a different story.

"I know what you mean about children changing as they get older," she said quietly, almost whispering. "But the saddest thing is that some children don't get to grow up at all." She stood up abruptly and went to her room.

"What's that all about?" Dan asked with a puzzled look on his face. "I thought you said she never had any kids."

"She didn't. But she did have a baby who died—stillborn. That was so many years ago, I'd forgotten." Sometimes I amazed myself with how smoothly I could lie.

Dan's eyes moistened and he shook his head sadly. "Poor thing. She would have been a great mom, too. Just look how good she is with our kids."

I didn't trust myself to answer, just nodded in mock agreement. It was truly astonishing how easy it was to fool Dan. He wasn't stupid, just naive. I guess if I'd grown up in a normal family like his, I'd think the best of others, too. But maybe the one good thing Mama had given me was the ability to see through peoples' masks into their true selves. That kind of knowledge was power.

"I'm going up to tuck Amelia in," I said calmly. "Why don't you go in the family room with the girls? They always sit too close to the TV if they're not reminded."

He chuckled at my concern and got up. He made no secret of the fact that he thought I was a worrywart. Well, somebody had to be one.

I slowly walked up the stairs. Amelia's door remained firmly closed, daring me to approach. I took a deep breath and opened it. I don't believe in knocking on your children's doors—they shouldn't have any secrets from their parents.

Amelia wasn't in bed. Instead, she was seated at her desk, busily writing in a notebook. When I came in, she stuffed it in a drawer.

"What are you writing, Amelia? I thought you didn't have any homework." I walked over to her with my hand out. "Let me see."

She reached in the drawer and pulled out a notebook. Was it the same one? I couldn't be sure.

"I was just rewriting my spelling words. There were some hard ones this week." She looked up at me blandly. Sure enough, the notebook contained a list of words, written three times each.

I sat down on the end of her bed and patted the spot next to me. "Come and sit here. We need to talk."

She warily moved to the bed and sat rigidly beside me. She was once again in her invisibility mode, head down and hair covering her face. I knew that posture because I had done the same thing as a child.

"Sometimes grownups say confusing things. Sometimes it

even sounds like they're angry with each other, when really they're just disagreeing. Do you understand what I'm saying?"

Amelia remained still, not betraying herself with a nod or a shrug. Her silence infuriated me. I grabbed her face by the chin and forced her to look at me.

"I asked you a question. Do not disrespect me by ignoring it."

Although she was looking straight at me, her eyes were unreadable. "Yes, ma'am. I understand about grownups."

I released my grip and stood up. "Well, that's good. I'm glad we cleared things up. You know you can come to me any time you have questions about anything—anything at all. I'm your mother, and I love you. You can trust me to give you the right answers. Not like some other people."

Amelia's head was bowed again, and she spoke in such a low tone that I barely heard her. "Like Aunt Mae, you mean."

"Exactly." I smiled to myself. She was a bright little girl. She'd seen through Mama, all right. I kissed the top of her head.

"Good night, little one. Sleep tight."

I turned the light out as I left her room. How long should I wait before she was sound asleep? I was pretty bright myself—and I knew there was a second notebook stashed in her desk drawer.

# CHAPTER SEVENTEEN

My eyes flew open when I heard the shower turn on. Damn! I'd only meant to lie down for a minute, but I'd ended up sleeping the whole night through. The "flu"—poisoning, for those who had eyes to see—must have taken a lot more out of me than I'd realized. Now I'd missed my window of opportunity to search for Amelia's notebook. I knew how crafty she was. She had undoubtedly hidden it somewhere else as soon as I left her room last night.

I sat up as Dan wandered into the bedroom, wrapped in his terrycloth robe. He came and sat on the end of the bed.

"Feeling better, hon? You slept like a log last night." He patted my feet.

"Yes, I'm almost a hundred percent. But, I'm just not sure . . ." I let my voice trail off weakly.

"Take another day. Lord knows you have enough sick time stored up. You're never absent. You were pretty darn sick. The school won't fall apart if you miss one more day." He chuckled and got up to get dressed.

I reached for the phone and called substitute services, then left a message at the school. Dan was right—the school wouldn't fall apart if I missed a day, but my family might disintegrate if I didn't stay home and do some investigating.

I waited until Dan left for work before getting out of bed. Mama had done her part again by getting the girls ready for school, and they left with their daddy. As soon as I heard the door slam, I leaped out of bed and went straight to Amelia's room.

I was just getting started on my search when I heard Mama come up the stairs. I quickly began stripping the bed.

"Honey, what are you doing up? You should be taking it easy." She looked at me with a false smile.

"Oh, you know me. I have a hard time doing nothing. I just thought I'd throw in a load of laundry."

"You know I'd be more than happy to do it for you, darlin' girl."

"No!" I cut her off quickly. "I mean, that's so kind of you, but I'm fine. It doesn't take much energy to turn on a washing machine."

Mama stiffened a bit, then put back on her phony smile. "Well, sugar, if you're sure you're all right, I'm gonna run a few errands—that is, if I can borrow your car for a little while."

I turned and faced her full on, clutching the sheets to my chest. "What kind of errands, Mama?"

"I just need to pick up a few things, maybe stop at the hairdresser's for a trim—you know. And then I'll be meeting a friend for lunch." She threw that last sentence out as if it were no big deal.

"Mama!" I dropped the sheets and walked toward her. "You don't know anyone here. Who the"—I stopped to catch my breath—"who are you having lunch with?"

She slid her eyes away from my gaze. "Well, you know how friendly I am, sugar. Why, I can strike up a conversation with the devil himself! Not that Ted is a devil—far from it. He's just the nicest man, with the most dreamy blue eyes, and—"

"Mama," I said threateningly. Left to her own devices, she could manipulate and twist the truth all day. The devil himself indeed! Takes one to know one, I guess.

"If you must know," she replied snippily, "I met him at the

grocery store. He's a perfect gentleman, and he has asked me to lunch."

"Let me guess," I said as I sat down on Amelia's bed. "He was wearing a Rolex, Bruno Magli shoes, and had a Mercedes in the parking lot."

"As a matter of fact, missy, it was a Movado watch, Ferragamo sandals, and a Prius. He's not the flashy type." She tried to keep a straight face and then burst out laughing. "Oh, darlin', you know me too well. I've always been attracted to the finer things in life."

I thought fast. If Mama had a sugar daddy on the string, that meant she'd be out of our lives in the blink of an eye. On the other hand, I would be unleashing her on an unsuspecting man who had no idea of what was in store for him.

It didn't take me long to decide. "Go ahead and take the car, Mama. But please be careful. You don't have a driver's license, and if anything happens, Dan would have my head—and yours, too."

"Don't you worry. I've always been a good driver. Besides, the café is just a few blocks away, right by the shopping center. So I can get my errands done and meet Ted in plenty of time." She reached down and gave me a hug. "Thank you so much, sugar. I'll tell you all about it when I get home." She bustled out of the room, humming to herself.

I stood up slowly and gathered the bed linens again. Best to wait until Mama was out of the house before I searched the room. I wasn't sure how Amelia was feeling about her right now, but I knew that Mama still counted on my eldest as an accomplice in whatever despicable schemes she might concoct.

After an interminable time spent listening to Mama fuss in the bathroom, humming and singing (I caught the lyrics of "Hey Good Lookin' "), she was finally gone. I had gone back to my room, pleading exhaustion, so I wouldn't have to talk to her anymore. She called out a cheery "bye-bye" and the house was finally silent. I hurried into Amelia's room to continue my investigation.

Where to begin? I decided on her desk, on the off chance that she hadn't removed the notebook. I pulled open the first drawer and gasped in dismay. It was full to bursting with scraps of paper, broken pencils, and who knew what else. Hadn't I taught her anything about keeping things in order? It was just another symptom of her rebelliousness. "Tidy drawers, tidy mind," I murmured to myself as I got busy.

Thirty minutes later I was finished with the desk and the dresser. I had nothing to show for my work, but I had left everything better than I found it. I glanced down at the floor where I had deposited the pile of junk from her newly cleaned drawers. Ticket stubs, crumpled drawings, broken jewelry—I really had no idea Amelia was such a packrat. I didn't feel up to tackling the closet yet, so I got down on my knees and looked under the bed. Nothing there but one slipper—the one she claimed had "disappeared." Sitting back on my heels, I thought. Where had I hidden my secrets when I was a girl?

It came to me in a flash. I pulled her mattress off the bed and there it was—the notebook. I picked it up carefully as though it might break. This book could unlock the secrets of my daughter's sullen attitude, lack of respect, and stubbornness. With any luck, it would also tell me just how much she knew—or imagined she knew—about Mama and me.

# CHAPTER EIGHTEEN

The notebook seemed to burn my hand as I carried it downstairs. I carefully tucked it into my knitting basket beside my favorite wing chair in the living room. A cup of tea was what I needed, I decided. I had just bought some Earl Grey and it was calling to me. A part of me knew that I was putting off reading Amelia's secret thoughts, but I firmly pushed my uneasiness to the back of my consciousness.

I went to the kitchen and started brewing the tea. Dan had bought me a beautiful bone china tea set for last Mother's Day, and I loved using it. The whole ritual of making tea calmed me. I had nothing to be ashamed of in reading Amelia's journal. After all, as her mother it was my duty to make sure she was not taking the wrong path. If she wouldn't confide in me, then I'd just have to take matters into my own hands.

Finally I was settled comfortably in the overstuffed chair, my cup of tea on a coaster on the lamp table. I reached into my knitting basket and took out the notebook. I figured that I could quickly stuff it out of sight if anyone came home unexpectedly.

*Monday September 9—It's the first day of school. I'm excited to see my friends but I know Mommy is going to talk to my teacher and embarrass me. She always tells my teachers how smart I am and that I'm just lazy when it comes to math. I wish—*

I paused in my reading and gazed unseeingly at the seascape on the wall opposite me. Embarrassed? By me? But that was how I felt when I was Amelia's age. She had no reason to be ashamed of my concern for her welfare. All I wanted was for her to grow up to be a successful adult. She didn't have to put up with the things I'd endured with Mama.

I groped for the teacup and brought it to my lips, then grimaced as I realized it was cold. Reading Amelia's words brought up a whirlwind of emotions. Clutching the notebook, I remembered.

*"Where are we going again, Mama?" I shifted my sweaty legs against the rough leather of the bus seat. I could feel drips of perspiration slowly rolling down my neck.*

*"I told you a million times—Mississippi. Now hush. Mama's thinking." She was probably too tired and hot to get very angry with me, I thought. I'd never seen her look so wilted.*

*She'd sprung this trip on me yesterday afternoon. I came home from school and found her tossing things in an old brown suitcase.*

*"Take what you need for a few weeks and put them in your backpack. We're going on an adventure."*

*"An adventure? Where? Why? Is Matt coming with us? Is he back?" My stepdad had left in the middle of the night about a week after Nathan died. Mama said he'd only cared about Nathan, not us, and that's why he left. I wasn't so sure. He'd always been kind to me, and I remembered how tight he hugged me when we were both crying about Nathan. I kept hoping he'd come back. It was weird how both my dads had taken off like that, without a word.*

*Mama snorted as she stopped packing and tucked her red curls behind her ears. "Not likely. We've seen the last of him, and good riddance. No, baby, it's gonna be a girls-only trip. You'll love Mississippi. It's so much prettier than this dirty old desert. There's the river, and magnolia trees, and—well, you'll see." She stuffed some lingerie into the suitcase and slammed it shut. "What are you staring at? Get busy! Our bus leaves in an hour."*

*I quickly gathered up a few changes of clothes and a couple of books, carefully putting them in my backpack. "But Mama, what about school? Finals are next week. If I miss them, I might fail the whole grade." I knew this was unlikely—my grades were so good that the final exams were only a formality. I just wanted to try to put up some sort of objection.*

*"You're smarter than anybody in that school, including most of the teachers. I'd like to see them try and hold you back!" She glared at me fiercely. "Now quit trying to waste time and get moving."*

*I knew when I was beaten. I went into my room and put a few more treasures in the backpack—my secret journal, a broken necklace my real dad gave me for my fifth birthday, a picture of Mama and Matt when they got married. Looking over my shoulder, I then picked up my most precious possession of all—Nathan's silky little baby blanket. Mama would screech like a banshee if she saw me with it, so I stuffed it down into the very bottom of my backpack.*

*"I'm ready," I said, walking back into the living room. Mama was sitting on the couch, counting a big stack of bills. She quickly tucked them into her purse and gave me a dazzling smile.*

*"All right! Let's blow this pop stand, sugar! You are going to absolutely love Mississippi. You'll get to meet lots of family there, too. Cousins, aunts, uncles, my mama"—a cloud passed over her face—"well, just lots of wonderful people. Southerners are much more refined than these dusty old desert folks. You'll see, you'll love it."*

*So here we were, on an interminable bus ride that seemed like it was going straight to hell. The air-conditioning was broken, and the gas fumes that seeped in through the floor made me feel sick to my stomach. Every now and then the bus would stop to let some people off and others on, but we only got off long enough to grab some vending machine snacks and sodas. Then it was right back on the uncomfortable seats and watching the drab scenery out the windows.*

*I tried to read, but the bouncy ride made the print jump and hurt my eyes, so I gave up. Mama didn't seem to want to talk, which was not like her at all. She was adding up some long columns of numbers, and every now and then a satisfied smile would cross her face. She saw me watching her and tucked the paper into her purse.*

*"You'd best try and get some sleep. We've still got a ways to go. You don't want to be all worn out when we get there."*

*I closed my eyes obediently, but my thoughts were too jumbled to let me sleep. Why had I never heard about these southern relatives before? Would they be happy to see us? Would we stay with them, or in a hotel? I'd never stayed in a hotel before. Maybe this would be a real adventure after all. Maybe this time I could trust Mama to make everything turn out all right. And then, in spite of myself, I fell asleep.*

I shook my head to get the unpleasant memories out of my brain. There was a lot about Mississippi that I didn't want to remember. I reopened Amelia's notebook and impatiently leafed through the blathering about school friends, unfair rules and favorite singers, until I got closer to the end. Here it was—her thoughts about me and Mama (Aunt Mae to her).

*Aunt Mae can be so cool sometimes, but other times I just don't get her. And she acts real sweet to Mommy, but Mommy seems like she doesn't really like her. Why? I heard them argu- ing last night, and I think—*

The next line was scratched out so thoroughly that I couldn't read it. That sneak! She must have guessed that I'd try to read this at some point. I threw the notebook down into the knitting basket and stood up. Glancing at the grandfather clock, I re- alized it was almost time for Dan and the kids to get home. What was taking Mama so long? If she wasn't home with the car soon, there'd be a problem.

I took my tea cup into the kitchen to wash up. Suddenly I

stopped in mid-track. Amelia would know as soon as she got home that I'd searched her room. Not only would her notebook be gone, but everything was neat and clean. I just couldn't help myself from tidying things up—the mess in her drawers and closet were like a personal affront to me.

Then I smiled as I thought of how it would play out. She wouldn't want to admit that she kept a secret journal, and I wouldn't mention it either. I'd just casually throw out that I'd straightened up her room because I was home today and wait for her reaction. This could actually be fun in a strange sort of way.

I had just finished washing the tea things and putting them away when I heard my car pull into the drive. Thank heavens Mama was home before Dan. He liked her, but he was a stickler about some things—like driving without insurance or a license. I guess it had something to do with being a dentist and having to carry malpractice insurance.

She had just breezed through the door when Dan and the girls drove up. I went to the door to greet them. This, I thought, is going to be good.

# CHAPTER NINETEEN

Mama elbowed me out of the way and hugged the girls first. "Baby girls!" she trilled. "Guess what I did today!"

Typical, I thought. It's always about her. She didn't think to ask them about their days. I stepped out from behind her and pushed my way into the hug.

"How did your spelling test go, Amelia? And Amanda, did you do a good job with your letters today? Abigail, did you get a green light today? You followed the rules, didn't you?"

Dan stood back from the melee. "Whoa, ladies," he said, with his hands up in a time-out signal. "Let 'em breathe, why don't you? Come on girls, go on in and get your snack."

"Remember to wash up first," I couldn't resist adding. The girls rushed upstairs and the three of us slowly followed them inside.

Dan gave me a quick kiss on my forehead. "Feeling better?" he asked tenderly. I nodded and leaned against him. He put his arm around me. It gratified me that he paid attention to me before turning to Mama.

"So, Aunt Mae," he said with a somewhat false joviality, "what was so absolutely awesome about your day today?"

Mama preened a bit before she answered. "Well, as a matter of fact, I had lunch with the nicest gentleman today, and he has asked me out to dinner tomorrow night. He said I was the most delightful person he's met since he moved to this little town."

Dan's eyebrows lifted in surprise, but he quickly covered his shock. "I didn't realize you'd had the opportunity to meet anyone. I mean, you always seem to be here at the house."

I couldn't hold back any longer. "Yes, Aunt Mae, it's caught me a little off guard, too. I mean, you and Uncle"—I scanned my memory for the name of her fake dead husband—"Phil were so devoted. You always said that he was the only one for you." I smiled sweetly as she glared at me.

Before she could open her mouth to reply, the girls came downstairs and I took them into the kitchen for their after-school snack. As usual, the two littlest ones chattered away about school and friends, while Amelia galumphed along behind, silent and moody. I glanced at her. "Oh, by the way, sweetie, I straightened up a few things in your room today. Really, I thought I taught you better. It's as if you have no respect for your possessions—and that makes it seem as if you have no respect for me."

I thought I heard some sort of snort come from Amelia, but I turned around just a tad too late to catch her at it. She looked blandly at me, not saying a word.

I busied myself with getting the raw vegetables out of the refrigerator. The girls sat down at the kitchen table, ready to eat.

"Oh, sweet things, I got you all some special treats today!" Mama came blowing in with a plastic grocery bag clutched in her hand. "Jess-girl, remember how you used to love Little Debbie snack cakes? Why, you used to pester me like all get out—"

"Now, Aunt Mae, the few times you visited, you might have bought me some junk food, but most of the time my *real* mother made sure I ate much more healthily. We'll put these in the freezer and keep them for a special treat." I grabbed the bag from her and quickly wrapped it up in a freezer bag. "There, done is done," I said brightly as I shoved the glutinous mess of preservatives into the freezer. All three girls were staring at Mama and me with big eyes.

"Well I never!" sputtered Mama as she spun around and almost ran to her room. I couldn't stop a little chuckle from escaping my lips.

Too bad I didn't, because I had not realized that Dan was standing in the kitchen doorway, a troubled look on his face. He gave me a look that meant "we need to talk" and turned away, carrying the newspaper with him into the family room.

I winced. It looked like I'd been taking Dan's good nature for granted. Usually he was so easy to handle that I'd become sloppy. It was all Mama's fault! Why couldn't she just disappear!

"We're all done, Mama," said Amanda. "The carrots were extra good today."

Abigail nodded in agreement. "I just *love* veggables," she pronounced, looking up at me with an anxious smile. Amelia sneered but said nothing.

"Okay, homework time. Bring your backpacks in here so we can get started. Oh, Amelia, could you just help me wash up before you get your things?"

Amelia looked in astonishment at me. I rarely asked for her help in the kitchen. She just wasn't as careful about things as I was, so it was usually easier to simply do things myself.

"Well, can't you even speak to me?" I stood with my hands on my hips, but a smile on my face.

"Yes, Mama. I'd be happy to help," she droned lifelessly, picking up the veggie tray and carrying it to the sink.

I followed her and stood close to her, so she had to look at me. I lowered my voice to an intimate whisper. "We have a few things to discuss, young lady. I know what you've been up to."

She started, a look of shock in her eyes. "Wh-what do you mean?"

"You know what I mean. And now that I'm onto you, don't

think you'll be getting away with it anymore. I'll be watching you like a hawk, young lady. And you know what a hawk is, don't you? It's a predator." I kept my voice low and bent down and grabbed her arms. "Don't test me."

I let go of her and straightened up. "Now go get your homework, sweetie. I want to see how that math is coming along," I said in a normal tone of voice.

She gave me a frightened glance and scampered up the stairs. It was almost too easy to intimidate her. There was no sport in fighting an unarmed opponent. She hadn't challenged my silly insinuations at all. In fact, she probably thought I was omniscient just because I was her mother.

I shook my head as I rinsed the vegetable tray and absently dried it off. When I was Amelia's age, I already knew that I could outsmart my mother. I knew just how to handle her. Poor little Amelia had a lot to learn.

# CHAPTER TWENTY

It was after dinner and the girls were upstairs getting ready for bed. Mama had not graced us with her presence all night—sulking in her room, no doubt. I had just finished loading the dishwasher when Dan walked into the kitchen.

"Jess, we need to talk. I'm picking up some strange vibes between you and Aunt Mae, and I want to know just what's going on. You begged me to let her move in, after all. I think I deserve an explanation for all the negativity the two of you zing at each other." He stood behind me with a solemn expression on his face.

"Oh honey, you know how we women can be," I said, ruffling his hair. "It's really no big deal, but we can talk about it later—after the girls are in bed."

He nodded and went back into the den. I heard the rustle of the newspaper as he settled into the recliner.

As I finished up in the kitchen, I plotted out the rest of the evening. Make Dan a nightcap, put on his favorite teddy, and he'd forget all about talking. I'd just have to be a little more careful about how I spoke to Mama when Dan was around. No biggie.

I dried my hands and went upstairs to check on the girls and tuck them in. After a quick reminder about tooth brushing, the two little ones hopped into bed with no problem. I stiffened as I entered Amelia's room. It wasn't that she intimidated me, it just took so much effort to deal with her.

"Night-night, sweetie," I said in a bright voice. "Clean face, clean teeth?"

"Yes, Mama. I remembered to cut my nails, too."

"Good girl. They were getting a little raggedy. Time to get in bed—and remember, you can only read for thirty minutes, then it's lights out."

"Okay. Umm, Mama?" Her face looked up pleadingly at me.

"Yes?"

"I—I love you."

I stepped back in surprise. Amelia hadn't said anything like that to me for quite some time.

"Do you love me, Mama? I'll try harder to be good, I promise." She reached out as though to take my hand.

I patted her head. "Of course, silly. All mothers love their little girls," I said, banishing the thought of Mama from my mind. "Now, get in bed. You have a math test tomorrow, remember." I turned and walked out of her room without looking back.

The rest of the evening went just as I planned. I mixed Dan one of his favorite dirty martinis—heavy on the gin—and then distracted him with some bedroom games. By the time he fell asleep, with a fatuous grin on his face, he'd forgotten all about talking.

I looked at my reflection in the mirror as I rubbed in my night cream. Just hang on for a little longer, I told myself. Mama will be gone soon enough, and then things will be back to normal. I crawled into bed and fell into a deep, dreamless sleep.

The next morning was our usual weekday rush. Mama did show up for breakfast, sitting at the table like a queen expecting her servants to wait on her. Mindful of my new resolve to put on a better show for Dan, I smiled brightly at her.

"I'm making waffles, Aunt Mae. How many would you like?"

She looked at me suspiciously. "None, thank you. I'll just have some juice. Teddy is taking me out to brunch later."

So now it's Teddy, I thought scornfully. Mama always was a fast mover. I poured her some juice without saying a word.

Eventually we all made it out the door with time to spare. Dan had given me an extra-passionate kiss before he jumped in his car. One problem down, a million to go. I smiled.

The day went surprisingly well. My students actually were glad to see me after dealing with an incompetent substitute. The hours flew by until it was time to pick up the girls and go home.

Mama met us as we walked in the door. She was beaming—practically glowing.

"You'll never guess what darling Teddy bought me!" she exclaimed, hugging all three girls at once. "Come see!" She led them into her room.

I followed, a knot in the pit of my stomach. My experience had always been that anything that made Mama happy usually meant trouble for me.

I heard it before I saw it, even over the excited oohs and aahs of the girls. The sound of chirps and trills needled their way through my brain. It was a bird! A dirty, filthy bird in my house! I gritted my teeth to keep from screaming.

Birds were among my least favorite of all living things. When I was little, a huge crow had attacked me as I played in the backyard. It was a miracle that I hadn't been scarred for life. Then, when I was a little older, I watched *The Birds* on TV. I was home alone, of course, and the frightening images of those horrible creatures swarming down on poor Tippi Hedren gave me nightmares for many years.

I took a deep breath. I didn't want to let my anxiety show. "Oh, Aunt Mae, how sad that you can't keep your little pet. You must have forgotten—or maybe you never knew—that I'm allergic to feathers. You'll just have to give it back to your friend."

Four crestfallen faces turned toward me. I allowed myself a quick glance at the cage with the flash of yellow inside. I didn't dare look at it straight on.

"But Jess-girl, he's such a pretty little thing. You won't even know he's here. I'll keep my door shut, and of course I'll be totally responsible for his care. Look how sad you've made the girls. You might not care how I feel, but think of your daughters. They deserve to have a pet."

All three girls looked at me with trepidation. They were trying to judge my mood. I decided to surprise them.

"Well, if you put it like that—" I said hesitatingly. You could have heard a pin drop in the room—that is, if that damned bird would quit squawking. I enjoyed having this power over their feelings—especially Mama's.

"Please, Mama?" whispered Amelia. Interesting. Both my mother and my daughter were enthralled with that little bunch of feathered germs. This could prove very useful.

"Okay," I said slowly. "But you've got to promise to keep your door closed all the time." I faked a sneeze. "I really am allergic, you know. Now girls, it's time for snacks and homework."

"Can't they stay in my room for just a little longer? I need their help in thinking of a name." Mama was back to her bubbly self.

"Ten minutes, and then I want to see you at the kitchen table. And don't forget to wash your hands. Birds carry all sorts of diseases." I turned to leave the room, but not before I saw Mama rolling her eyes and the girls stifling giggles. It didn't bother me a bit. I could wait.

# CHAPTER TWENTY-ONE

The next few days passed unremarkably. The girls all spent quite a bit of time in Mama's room, carrying on with that damned bird. They'd decided to name it Sunshine, because Mama said he brought "a little bit of sunshine into a dreary world." Gag. She kept her part of the bargain, though. I never had to see the little miserable fluff ball and hardly even had to hear it.

One thing that brought some sunshine into my life was Mama's intensifying relationship with good old Teddy. I had yet to meet him, but he was quickly becoming one of my favorite people. Because of Teddy, Mama was out several nights a week, almost always missing dinner with the family. Life, in many ways, seemed almost normal again. The two little girls would ask when Auntie Mae would be back, but it was easy to redirect them into other activities. Amelia, though, became more withdrawn than ever. When Mama was home, Amelia would follow her like the proverbial shadow. Sometimes Mama would fuss over her and pay her a lot of attention, but more often she would go on and on about all of the great places Teddy was taking her and almost ignore Amelia altogether. I knew what that felt like.

Thursday night rolled around and I decided to up the ante. This relationship of Mama's needed to be pushed to the next level.

"Aunt Mae," I said sweetly as we sat around the table, finishing our apple pie. "Why don't you invite Teddy over for dinner on Sunday? We'd all love to meet this wonderful man who's monopolizing all of your time."

Dan chimed in. "Yeah, Aunt Mae. I think that's a great idea. After all," he added, with a mischievous glint in his eyes, "I need to make sure his intentions are honorable."

"Oh you," tittered Mama. "Well, I guess I could see if he's free Sunday. What do you think, girls? Would you like to meet my big ol' Teddy bear?"

Amelia nodded, somewhat unenthusiastically, but Amanda and Abigail squealed in excitement. "Yes, yes, yes!" shrieked Amanda, with Abigail quickly following with, "Is he really a teddy bear, Aunt Mae? I thought he was a regular person."

A trill of laughter came from Mama. "You are so cute! He's a real person, all right. A real"—she paused and just barely licked her lips—"man."

Honestly. Here she was, an old lady who by all rights should be content to stay home and knit, and she was acting like a hot-to-trot teenager. I swallowed my revulsion and spoke.

"Okay, then, it's settled. Is there anything special he'd like for dinner? What about prime rib?"

"My goodness, that's so extravagant! But if it wouldn't be too much trouble—"

"Not at all, Aunt Mae. I insist that you let me do all the cooking. After all, you'll be busy entertaining your date."

She leaned over and kissed me on the cheek. "You are just the sweetest thing, Jess-girl. You've always been the kind of person who just gives, gives, gives. Just like me. It must run in the family."

I wanted nothing more than to wipe my cheek clean, but I forced myself to smile. "Yes, Aunt Mae, you're probably right."

I glanced at Dan and saw him beaming at the two of us. Oh well, a bit of fakery could go a long way in buying some marital peace.

It was Sunday night, and Mama was fluttering around the house just like that damned bird. In fact, she was even wearing a yellow dress. She smoothed the couch cushions, tweaked the blinds, and generally drove me crazy with her fussiness. I gritted my teeth and continued to stir the Hollandaise sauce that was going to be paired with the fresh asparagus.

"Jess-girl," she warbled behind me, almost causing me to drop my spoon. "How's dinner coming?"

"Just fine, if you'll leave me alone long enough to finish."

She pouted prettily. "Now, don't be like that. After all, if things go well with Teddy and me, I could be out of your hair in two shakes of a lamb's tail."

I whirled around, startled by her discernment. "Why— why—" I sputtered.

"Let's not pretend, Jess. I know it's driving you crazy to have me here—although I don't begin to understand why. I am your mother, after all. And we were so close when you were little. I sacrificed for you. I took care of you—"

"Enough!" I slammed the spoon down. "Let's not act like we were some *Leave it to Beaver* family. We both know the truth. And yes, I'd love to see you get together with Teddy and move on with your life. If you'll just give me five minutes to myself, I'll put a dinner on the table that will knock his socks off—and I don't care if you tell him you made every morsel with your own lily-white hands. Just get out of the kitchen and leave me alone."

She looked at me strangely, then gave a mock salute. "Okay, general. Whatever you say." She whirled around and flounced out of the room.

Six o'clock finally came, and there was a knock on the door at exactly that time—not a minute before, not a minute after. Dan, the kids and I sat expectantly in the living room while Mama rushed to answer it. When she got there, she paused for a moment, touched her hair, and threw open the door.

"Teddy!" she cried, giving him a big hug. "Come in and meet my family!"

A tall, silver-haired man emerged from her arms and strode over to shake our hands. He carried himself with military precision.

"Hello, Dan, Jessie. I've heard great things about you from Mae. And these three lovely ladies must be Amelia, Amanda, and Abigail." He flashed his white teeth in an engaging smile. "Don't quiz me on who's who until the end of the evening, though."

I excused myself to get drinks and appetizers. As I arranged the cream cheese pinwheels on the platter, I kept an ear cocked to hear as much of the conversation in the other room as I could. There was something about Teddy—maybe the way he stood, his air of confidence, something that—of course! I'd bet my life that he'd either been in the military or served on a police force. As a girl, I'd been able to spot a policeman from miles away—just a little bonus from living with Mama. Now that could be a problem. He seemed enamored of Mama for the moment, but what if he decided to do a background check? That's what single people did nowadays. I was in a quandary. As much as I'd love seeing Mama get her comeuppance, I also wanted her to move out and leave us alone. I sighed, picked up the serving tray, and called to Dan.

"Honey, could you help me with the drinks, please?"

He came bounding into the kitchen. "Wow, that Teddy is a great guy! He was just telling us about his time in the FBI. I bet he's full of stories."

I nodded and tried to keep my smile pasted on, although my lips were trembling. FBI! It was worse than I thought.

# CHAPTER TWENTY-TWO

Despite my misgivings, dinner went well. Mama was always at her best when she had her claws in an unsuspecting male, and Teddy was more than a match for her in the charm department. He entertained us with funny stories from his past FBI work, including inside looks at some pretty famous people. He managed to include everyone in the conversation, even little Abigail.

"Hey there, little miss," he said, tugging gently on one of her pigtails. "Is this too much grown-up talk for you? Why don't you tell us something you learned in school today?"

Abigail brightened and sat up straight. "I learned a song," she said proudly.

"Well, let's hear it then. Stand up and sing, baby girl." Mama's tone was a little impatient. She did so hate to have the spotlight off her.

My little girl pushed her chair back and stood up. She smoothed her dress and then clasped her hands in front of her. I saw Amelia rolling her eyes at the theatrics of her younger sister, but no one else seemed to notice so I bit my tongue.

"A peanut sat on the railroad track,

"His heart was all a-flutter,

"Around the bend came number ten,

"Choo-choo peanut butter!"

Everyone laughed and clapped—even Amelia—but I had to force my smile. That song brought back memories—bad ones. I hadn't thought of Cousin Sally and Grandma for years. I glanced at Mama. She was laughing along with everyone else. It was obvious that the silly little song meant nothing to her. What must it be like, I thought, to be able to push all your evil deeds out of your head and live as though they'd never happened? If only I could forget half as easily.

I quickly got up and went to get dessert, homemade strawberry shortcake. It seemed like a nice light ending to the heavy prime rib meal. I quickly whipped the fresh cream and dolloped it on each individual dish. That damned song kept running through my mind. I started mentally repeating the names of the states and capitals. This was a trick I'd learned as a young girl when there were things I was trying not to think about. Sometimes I had to get all the way to Cheyenne, Wyoming, and then start all over again.

"How did you know this is my favorite dessert, Jess? This whole dinner has been fantastic. I tell you, Dan, you'd better treat her right. She's a keeper." Teddy dug into his shortcake with relish.

Dan beamed, nodded, and turned his attention to dessert also. Mama sat there steaming, fiddling with her fork, and finally spoke up.

"You know, Teddy, I was all set to cook for you but Jess insisted on doing everything herself. She can be a bit bossy that way." She said this with a smile that was as false as her hair color.

I smiled just as phonily. "Yes, I do enjoy being queen of my kitchen. I've been like that since I was a girl." I shot a venomous look at Mama. She had been in the kitchen so rarely while I was growing up that I'd been forced to learn to cook for self-preservation.

Mama ignored me. "Why don't I come over to your place one night and cook for you, Teddy? I'm sure I could think of something you'd like." She winked broadly as he blushed.

I could feel the strawberries rise up in my throat. Had she no shame? I was so done with her. I felt sorry for Teddy, but if he was stupid enough to fall into her trap, it would be all the better for me and my family.

I thought the night would never end, but finally Teddy took his leave, Mama retired to her room, and the girls were in bed. Dan was full of chatter about Teddy and what a great guy he was. I tried just nodding and smiling in response, but he could tell I wasn't really into the conversation.

"What's up, Jess? Don't you like Teddy? He acts like he really cares for Aunt Mae. They seem perfect for each other."

"Mmm, you're probably right. I just have a bit of a headache. Sorry, sweetie. I guess I wasn't paying attention."

Dan was immediately contrite that he hadn't noticed my discomfort. He smoothed my pillow, tucked me in, and brought me some water and an aspirin. He went into the bathroom and closed the door so that he wouldn't disturb me as he prepared for bed.

I closed my eyes, willing myself to sink into a dreamless sleep. But like so many other times in my life, I didn't get what I wanted.

*I opened my eyes as the bus stopped. Mama pushed me in front of her as we got off. It seemed like huge clouds of steam surrounded us. I coughed.*

*"Better get used to it, sugar," said Mama. "Mississippi in the summer time is no place for the faint of heart." She grabbed my shoulder and stood there, looking around as though she were expecting someone.*

*"Huh," she snorted. "I shoulda known. We'll have to hoof it."*

*The walk seemed to take forever. There were big trees leaning in on us ominously, and thick clouds of gnats swarming in front of our faces. I dragged our suitcase behind me, and it kept bumping my legs.*

*Bump—swat the bugs—bump—swat the bugs. I was in a monotonous routine.*

*Suddenly a big gray house loomed up ahead. Mama stopped so abruptly that I almost collided with her.*

*"There it is, sugar," she said. "Home sweet home." Her voice dripped with sarcasm.*

*The next thing I knew I was sitting at a Formica table, drinking a glass of tepid milk and trying not to gag. Mama and someone she'd introduced as Grandma were talking in the next room, their voices raised. I tried to block out the ugly words I was hearing—"bitch," "ugly old whore," "nothing but a tramp." I put my hands over my ears and trembled.*

*"Hey," someone whispered. "That ain't gonna work. You gotta put some other words in your head."*

*I looked up and saw a little blond girl standing in front of me. She grinned broadly, showing the space where her two front teeth had been.*

*"I'll sing a song for you, but I gotta whisper. It's better if nobody notices us."*

*"Wh-who are you?" I stammered, blinking through my tears.*

*"I'm Sally. I reckon we're cousins. Here, hold my hand. You'll feel better." She straightened her shoulders and began to sing in a soft, clear voice.*

*"A peanut sat on the railroad track,*
*"His heart was all a-flutter.*
*"Around the bend came the number ten,*
*"Choo-choo, peanut butter!"*

*We both started giggling. Then I heard the scream. Everything went black.*

# Chapter Twenty-Three

I woke up with my head in a fog. Dan was still asleep, his face slack with just a bit of drool trickling out of his mouth. I gently stroked his hair. He was so good, so trusting. No matter what it took, I would not let Mama ruin the life I had struggled to build.

Glancing at the clock, I saw that it was only five thirty. Something terrible had awoken me, but I couldn't remember what. Just as well. Certain memories weren't meant to be disturbed. As long as I was awake, I might as well get up and start the day. Lolling in bed was not an option. It was this kind of discipline that had made me into the person I was today.

I took a quick shower, dressed and went downstairs. I glanced at Mama's closed bedroom door as I passed by on my way to the kitchen. Of course, *she* wouldn't be up for hours. Most of my childhood memories involved me getting myself up, dressed, and off to school without disturbing Mama's precious "beauty rest." My children had never experienced such a thing, and never would. I felt strengthened with my knowledge that I was doing the right thing in the right way.

Since I had extra time because of my early rising, I decided to make eggs Benedict. The girls were not overly fond of the dish, but Dan loved it and Mama would be jealous of my culinary ability. I was just giving the Hollandaise sauce an extra stir when Dan ambled in and engulfed me in a bear hug.

"Mmm, eggs Benny! What's the occasion?"

I forced myself to not snap at him for interrupting my cooking. I smiled and hugged him back.

"Just wanted to let my sweet husband know how much I appreciate him. Would you be a dear and make sure the girls are getting up? Breakfast will be ready in just a few."

He went off obediently and I breathed a small sigh of relief at being left in peace. I had just put the last plate on the table when he returned with the girls in tow. I looked critically at them to make sure they were presentable.

"Amelia, tuck in your blouse, please. Amanda, let me retie your bow. Abigail, show me your fingernails." They all submitted patiently to my inspection. They were used to it. Thank goodness, today all was well.

The girls sat down and began to eat, although not with Dan's enthusiasm. I thought I saw Amelia wrinkle her nose at the gourmet fare, but I wasn't sure. Left to their own devices, the girls would eat nothing but cold Pop-Tarts for breakfast.

Abigail looked up from her plate where she'd been busily stirring her egg so that it would look like she'd eaten it. "Mama, where's Auntie Mae? Is she with Teddy?"

"Of course not! She lives here, not with him. She's just catching up on her beauty sleep."

"But she's already boo—pretty. She doesn't need to sleep for that." Abigail had a bit of a lisp and tended to avoid words that accentuated it.

Before I could reply, Mama floated in garbed in a fuchsia peignoir. "I heard that, you sweet thing you! Auntie Mae loves you!"

Abigail beamed at her praise. Amanda was busy nibbling at the edges of her English muffin and seemed not to notice, but Amelia—Amelia shot her little sister a look of pure hatred. I gasped involuntarily. There was something about the look on her face—it was Mama to the core! Mama when she was her bad self. I quickly recovered and greeted my nemesis.

"Good morning, Aunt Mae. Did you sleep well?"

"Oh yes! I had the most delightful dreams of my Teddy! Isn't he just a doll?"

She chattered on as I sat silently. One thing, when Mama was in a room there was no pressure to carry the conversational load.

"Jess-girl, I swear you are the best cook. This breakfast is simply scrumptious. How do you do it?" I watched mesmerized as her sharp little teeth chewed the egg and Canadian bacon. She always did relish a good meal.

"Nothing to it, really. You probably don't remember, but my mother was a gourmet cook. She and I used to spend hours together in the kitchen, whipping up all sorts of delicacies." I spoke deliberately, hoping my words would sting.

I was disappointed. She hadn't really been listening. Big surprise. I sat fuming in silence, but suddenly something in her mindless prattle caught my attention.

"Sorry, Aunt Mae, what did you say?"

"I said, Teddy wants to take me out to the lake to see his boat. It's about a two-hour drive, I think. We're leaving about noon and we'll have dinner at the yacht club out there. So don't wait up for me!" She giggled like an overage school girl.

I nodded absently as my mind began to race. She'd be out of the house all afternoon and evening. Maybe I could use that time to my advantage.

With breakfast over and the kitchen clean, it was time for all of us to be off—all except Mama, that is. She'd waltzed back into her room to primp for her big day with Teddy. I could hear that bird from hell twittering as she opened her bedroom door.

I gave Dan a kiss as he left for his office, then hustled the girls into the car. I took advantage of the ride time to quiz Amelia on her math facts. She still stubbornly refused to take her schoolwork seriously. In the midst of this, Abigail began to hum her song from the night before.

"Abigail! Stop that at once, please! That song is just a silly piece of fluff! If you want to sing, there are many more meaningful songs to learn. I'll talk to your teacher about some more suitable tunes."

Abigail didn't speak, but her eyes brimmed with tears. I could see in the rearview mirror as she furtively wiped her eyes.

"Now now, tears don't solve anything. Let's go over the schedule for today. Abigail, you and Amanda have bell-ringing practice after school, and Amelia, you have piano. So you all need to be ready as soon as school's out so nobody will be late."

They all nodded as I pulled up to the elementary school where I worked and the girls attended class. I like to get there early enough that I have time to organize my day before my students arrive, so Amelia, Amanda, and Abigail go to early morning study hall. Many of the children who attend with them also eat breakfast at school, but of course my girls have a mother who cares enough to cook them a hot meal every morning.

The day proceeded almost without a hitch. We were prepping for state testing, and I pride myself on excelling at drill and practice. My scores were always among the highest in the district. I only had one student who wasn't responding correctly.

"Now, Jimmy, you don't want to disappoint me, do you? You know this letter, I know you do. What sound does it make?" I stood in front of his desk.

The little redhead looked up at me uncertainly. "Buh-buh-B?" he said hopefully.

I shook my head impatiently. "Jimmy, you're not trying. Think again."

The room was completely silent as he bit his lips and twisted his hands. "Puh-puh P?"

"Class, we have a student here who doesn't care about learning. He must not want to learn how to read. And if you can't read, what happens to you, boys and girls?" I looked out at the other twenty-four students sitting quietly in their seats. Finally, Marissa, one of my favorites, raised her hand. I nodded at her, giving her permission to speak.

"You end up a failure." Her voice rang clear and true.

"That's right. And we don't want that to happen to anyone here, do we?" The children all shook their heads solemnly.

"So, Jimmy, you'll stay in at recess today and we'll practice. Maybe this time you'll pay attention." The little boy slumped down and buried his head in his hands. I ignored him and went on with the rest of the lesson. Children responded to high expectations, and if they weren't getting them at home, then it was my job to provide them.

Soon enough the day was over and it was time to gather the girls and get them to their activities. I felt an odd exhilaration. I had a plan for how I was going to spend the afternoon alone at the house. It was time to ferret out some of Mama's secrets. Her room awaited.

# CHAPTER TWENTY-FOUR

I pulled into the driveway and shut off the car. The girls were at their after-school activities, Dan was at work, and Mama wouldn't be home until later that evening. I had at least an hour to investigate the she-devil's lair. I hurried into the house and went straight to her room.

Opening the door, I paused for a moment. I had decorated the guest room to my taste, but now it said Mama all over it. She had added some garish hot pink satin pillows on the bed, her peignoir trailed over the bedside chair, and the dresser was cluttered with bottles and jars. I walked over and picked one up. "Evening in Paris"—I should have known. That was always her favorite scent.

Before I could get started on my investigation, I was disturbed by the obnoxious twittering of Mama's pet puffball. I quickly covered the cage and it subsided with a few muffled peeps. I noticed feathers on the carpet under the cage. I couldn't stop myself from grabbing a tissue and picking them up. Maybe that would be a giveaway to Mama that someone had been in her room, but knowing her, she wouldn't even notice.

After throwing the errant feathers into the trash, I looked around the room. Where to begin? I took a cursory look into the dresser drawers—nothing out of the ordinary, unless you counted cheap lace lingerie as odd attire for a sixty-plus grandmother. Nothing was hidden under the drawer liners, so I moved on to the bed.

My heart began to beat a little quicker when I spotted a metal box under the bed. I pulled it out. Locked! The padlock seemed to stare at me mockingly. I had many talents, but lock picking was not among them. I tugged at the lock on the off chance that it hadn't been closed correctly, but it held fast. Then something struck me. I remembered buying a similar lock for Amelia last year. She had signed up for violin class at school and was required to provide a lock for the music closet. Of course, she hadn't stayed with the lessons, probably because I'd let her know how much it pleased me for her to branch out musically. But that was neither here nor there. She and I had argued over her insistence on keeping the sticker with the combination on the back of the lock. I told her it was foolish to leave access available to whomever wanted to take her violin, and she replied that she couldn't remember the combination and who'd want her stupid old violin anyway. I shook my head to clear my thoughts. That was in the past. Right now I had more important things to concentrate on.

I lifted the lock and almost laughed out loud. Like grandmother, like granddaughter. Mama had left the sticker on the back, too. It was a matter of moments to turn the dial and open the box.

It was full of papers. Placed right on top was her discharge from prison. I skimmed through it briefly. It stated that she had been a "model prisoner" and as such was recommended for early release. Model prisoner, my Aunt Fanny! She'd snowed them just as she had so many others in her life. But what was this? She had a parole officer! Surely she should have been checking in with this person. To my knowledge, no one had visited her or called except for dear old Teddy. This would bear further investigation.

Underneath the prison document was a packet of letters tied with a pink ribbon. I almost didn't want to look at them because the thought of reading her old love letters was enough to make me sick. Taking a deep breath, I picked them up—and immediately dropped them as though my hand had been scalded. They were all addressed to me.

I blinked and looked more closely at the envelopes. There were about twenty of them, and they bore the addresses of various foster homes I'd lived in. Each was stamped "No Forwarding Address—Return to Sender" in bold black print.

I began to shake uncontrollably. Just the sight of those addresses brought back horrible memories. That first placement, where the husband of the house—I wouldn't call him a father—had walked in on me repeatedly when I was dressing or getting ready to shower. The one where I was treated as a virtual slave, doing all of the housework and watching the younger children every day after school. The house where I had dared to hope I'd found a real home, only to be sent back to children's services one day with no explanation. My vision blurred and I slumped against the bed. I realized I was clutching the letters so tightly that they were creased in my hands. I quickly sat up and smoothed them until they looked as they had when I'd found them.

All those years, I'd thought she had cut me off. At first, it was painful, but then I was glad. With Mama out of my life, I could reinvent myself and be whoever I wanted to be. Gradually I had pushed the ugliness of my life into the farthest reaches of my mind, until I hardly remembered being "Jess-girl." That is, until Mama waltzed in and resurrected the past.

I slipped the first letter out of its envelope. What had she written to me, all those years ago? I unfolded the lined paper and began to read:

*My Dearest Daughter,*

*How I miss you! I wish—*

Before I could read any further, I heard the grandfather clock in the hall strike the hour. I was supposed to be picking the girls up right now! With a strangled sob, I put the letter back in the envelope, replaced everything in the box, relocked it, and shoved it under the bed. Now that I knew it was there, I could come back another time.

We had a relaxed family evening—no Mama to cause a fuss or suck all the attention onto herself. All three girls were amazingly compliant about homework and bedtime routines. I only had to remind Amelia once and Amanda twice to brush their teeth. Little Abigail did it all on her own even though she was the baby.

Once they were all in bed, I sat down beside Dan on the couch and pretended to watch some mindless TV show. Of course, my mind was completely preoccupied with the box in Mama's room. I began planning when I could get back in there and have more time when suddenly the front door flew open. Mama was back.

"Hello, dear ones! I have just had the most fabulous time! Teddy's boat is a-mazing! And dinner at the yacht club—I was treated like a queen, an absolute queen!"

Dan chuckled at her exuberance. I pasted a smile on my face. She swept into the room and paused dramatically.

"However, I am just wiped out, don't you know. The sun, the water—I swear I could fall asleep standing right here."

Dan stood up. "We can't let that happen. Teddy would never forgive us if we let any harm come to you! Here, let me take your jacket and you scoot right off to bed."

"Oh, Dan, I do hope Jess-girl knows what a gem you are! Ta-ta, all." I held my breath as she opened her bedroom door. Would she notice anything out of place? I thought I had been careful, but what if I forgot something? What if she noticed the feathers had been cleaned up? Wait—the cage cover! I'd thrown

115

it over to stop the incessant squawking, and in my rush to leave, I hadn't taken it off again. I groaned. This could be a problem.

A piercing shriek came from her room, followed by hysterical crying. Dan and I both jumped up and ran toward the incoherent gabbling.

"Ma—Aunt Mae, what is it?" I gasped. Dan rushed in and threw his arms around her.

"Calm down, Aunt Mae. What's wrong? What happened?" He held her close and her cries became more muffled. She suddenly pulled back and glared at me, hatred in her eyes.

"You!" she hissed. "You did this! You couldn't bear for me to be happy!"

"Wh-what are you talking about?" I knew this wasn't about me picking a few feathers off the carpet, or covering the cage of the little beast.

Without speaking, she pointed toward Sunshine's cage. The little bird was lying stiffly on the base of the cage. He was obviously dead.

# CHAPTER TWENTY-FIVE

I felt my heart beating out of my chest. I didn't have the breath to speak. I was sure the bird had been alive when I left, but could I really be certain? He'd shut up after I'd thrown the cover over his cage, and I hadn't checked on him—why would I?

The next thing I knew, Dan was leaning over me with a worried look on his face. I was lying on the couch with a pillow under my feet.

"Are you okay, honey? You took a header in there. You really scared me."

"I—I think so." I put my hand to my head. The wooziness had not completely gone away. "What happened?"

He looked nervous. "Well, Aunt Mae was so upset about Sunshine—I mean, she wasn't really making sense—and then, the next thing I knew—kablam. You were out cold on the floor. How's your head? You'll probably have a pretty good goose egg."

I gingerly lifted my head and felt the back of it. "I think you're right. Where's Aunt Mae?"

"Umm, she said she was going to call Teddy and have him pick her up. I guess she'll stay with him tonight. You stay here—I'll get an icepack for your head." He rushed away as though the fiends of hell were after him.

I slumped back down on the couch. This was not what I had planned at all. Certainly I wanted Mama out of the house, but not this way. I could tell Dan wasn't sure if I'd had something to do with the bird's death or not. Damn the woman! Animals died every day—it didn't mean they'd been murdered. She probably forgot to feed it or something. Based on her complete lack of mothering instincts, that seemed a more likely scenario than someone sneaking in and killing the dirty little bunch of feathers.

Dan returned with an icepack and gently placed it under my head. He'd even remembered to wrap it in a towel, so the couch cushions wouldn't get damp. I smiled gratefully at him. Maybe things weren't beyond repair.

I chose my words carefully. "So Sunshine is dead. Couldn't it be from natural causes? I mean, birds don't really live that long, do they?"

He refused to meet my eyes. "Well, I'm no vet, but I did take a look at him. It looked like—well, like his neck was broken."

Before I could reply, I heard Mama's bedroom door slam shut. Her footsteps echoed angrily on the wooden floor of the hall. Dan and I looked at each other. I reached for his hand, and thank God he took it.

She paused in the entryway off the living room and stood there like an avenging Fury. She looked at Dan and pointedly spoke to him alone.

"I'm going to wait for Teddy outside. I'll let you know what to do about my things. You're a good man, Dan. Please be careful." She sailed out the front door, carrying her small overnight bag.

I clutched Dan's hand convulsively. It was the only thing that kept me from jumping up and smacking her. How dare she make me the fall guy in this mess? It was just like her to avoid taking any responsibility.

Dan unlocked my fingers and flexed his hand. "Wow, honey, you've got quite a grip. Why don't you come up to bed now?

Here, let me help you." He reached out for me and pulled me off the couch.

I leaned into him as we made our way upstairs. My thoughts were flying around in my head like bats in a cave. The letters—the bird—Mama—I couldn't think clearly. I was suddenly so tired that I could barely keep my eyes open.

"Can I get you anything? How's your head?" Dan hovered over me anxiously as I sat down on the bed.

"I—I just need to sleep. I'll be all right." I sank back against the pillows and shut my eyes.

"Okay, then. I'll let you get some rest. I'm just going downstairs for a while—watch a little TV."

I nodded, turned over, and went to sleep.

*I was walking down a dimly lit hallway. There were doors along both sides, and I somehow knew that I shouldn't open them. Suddenly one to my left began to open on its own. I fearfully looked inside and saw a man sitting on a chair, his back to me. He stood up so abruptly that the chair was knocked over. He turned toward me. "Baby girl," he moaned, his hands outstretched. "Baby girl."*

*"D-daddy?" My voice sounded small. I began to run.*

*Another door opened, this one on my right. I stopped in front of it, my heart hammering in my chest. Inside the room, a man stood over a baby bed.*

*"Jess? Jess, can you help me?" He picked up a small bundle wrapped in a blanket and began to walk toward me.*

*I knew I didn't want to see what was in that bundle. I turned and fled down the long hall. Another door creaked open.*

*An old woman sat in a rocking chair with a young girl on her lap. The child appeared to be asleep. The old woman was crooning a song.*

*"A peanut sat—a peanut sat—a peanut sat."*

*"Stop it!" I screamed. "It wasn't my fault! I didn't know! It wasn't me!"*

*I looked frantically for a way out, but the walls of the corridor were closing in on me. I pushed against the wall nearest to me, gasping for breath. There was a noise behind me. I didn't want to turn around, but I couldn't stop myself.*

*They were all there, moving slowly toward me. Daddy, Matt and Nathan, Grandma and Sally. Their faces looked so sad.*

*"I'm sorry. I'm so sorry. Please forgive me," I whispered as I huddled down into a fetal position. "Please—".*

I woke up, clutching the blanket. I began to shake uncontrollably. Dan wasn't in bed beside me. I was alone, all alone. There was no one to take care of me but myself.

# Chapter Twenty-Six

Breakfast the next morning was a quiet affair. Dan sat behind his newspaper and then left early for work. I told the girls to be still because I had a terrible headache—and I did. I'd had very little sleep after my nightmare.

As I hustled my daughters out the door, I glanced down the hallway at Mama's door. It was still closed. A gruesome thought struck me. Had Dan cleaned up the bird? I shuddered to think it might still be in there, dead in its cage. Well, I couldn't do anything about it now. Another minute and we'd be late.

I was rushing into my classroom when a voice stopped me. I turned and saw Amy Blankenship, the school psychologist, waving her hand as she walked toward me.

"Yoo-hoo, Jess. Glad I caught you. We need to talk."

My insides turned to ice. What had Amelia been saying? Was she exhibiting some of Mama's behaviors? Had she been blabbing about things going on in our home?

I must have looked shocked, because she laughed and said, "Don't look so scared. I promise I'm not here to psychoanalyze you. Everybody thinks I spend all my time figuring out people's motives and behavior, but honestly, I get enough of that with the kids."

I forced a smile and surreptitiously wiped my wet hands on my skirt. "You just startled me, that's all. What can I do for you?"

"Well, you know little Jimmy in your class—the little carrot-top?"

I nodded impatiently. Now that it appeared she was not here about me or my daughter, I was in a hurry to get this conversation to the point.

"His parents have asked me to test him for possible learning disabilities. I have some observation forms here that I'll need you to fill out." She brandished a sheaf of papers at me.

"Learning disabilities?" I took the papers and glanced briefly at them. "Whatever gave them that idea? He's perfectly capable—just lazy."

"Now now, that's not politically correct. And we really won't know for sure until the testing's completed. I'll need these forms back ASAP. Thanks ever so." She turned and flounced off.

I sighed impatiently. One more thing to do—and so unnecessary. I could tell Amy Blankenship and Jimmy's parents exactly what was wrong. He was a lazy little boy who had no respect for authority. I shuddered to think what he must be like at home.

Of course, Amy wouldn't pick up on any of that. She loved to put labels on people. I'd had enough of that when I was growing up—case workers, psychologists, counselors—all of them asking me how I felt and why. As though they could ever understand.

It wasn't until the day was finally over and I was pulling into the driveway with the girls in tow that I remembered the bird episode. I glanced in the rearview mirror at my daughters.

"Girls, there's something I need to discuss with you. Aunt Mae has decided to move out. It will really be better for all of us, so I hope you'll be happy about it."

Three pair of stricken eyes stared back at me. Only Amelia was brave enough to speak, but what she said shocked me.

"Did you make her move, Mama? What did you do?" Her voice was angry.

I pushed down my rage. It wouldn't do to let her know she'd gotten to me. "Out of the car, all of you. Get started on your homework right away—no excuses."

The girls knew better than to argue when I used that certain tone. They scurried into the house and did as they were told. I followed more slowly. There was something I needed to do, and I wasn't looking forward to it.

I walked to Mama's room and stood staring at the door. Thoughts of the dead bird filled my mind. If Dan hadn't disposed of it, I would have to. I couldn't let that bundle of filth stay in my home. Why, it might have been diseased. Taking a deep breath, I pushed open the door.

"Hello, baby girl," said Mama calmly, sitting in front of her vanity. "How was your day?" She turned around and smiled at me, but not with her eyes. They held a look of steely hatred.

"I—I thought you were at Teddy's," I stammered.

"I just bet you did. Is that why you were coming into my room, because you thought I wouldn't be here? What was your plan this time? Steal something? Vandalize my belongings?"

"Of course not! I was just—just—" I couldn't stop myself from glancing at the empty cage.

"No, that's right. You've already done the most evil thing imaginable. Nothing else would hurt me as much."

She put down the hairbrush she'd been holding in her hand and stood up, facing me. Involuntarily, I took a step back.

"You listen to me, missy," she whispered in a menacing tone. "I care too much about this family to let you have your way with them. I'm staying right here so I can protect your sweet husband and those three darling girls from a mother who is out—of—control." She punctuated the last three words with pokes to my chest.

The physical contact roused me from my cowardly trance. I swatted her hands away.

"Don't you dare try to act the saint with me! My family needs protection, all right, but from you, not me! You've never cared about anyone but yourself a day in your life. I bet I know why you're back—Teddy threw you out! I knew he was too smart to be taken in by you for long."

My words about Teddy struck home, I could tell. Mama's shoulders slumped and she broke eye contact with me.

"He wanted me to stay—begged me to, in fact. But he's just in a little ol' bachelor pad, and things were so cramped."

I couldn't stop myself from laughing. "That's the best you can come up with? Oh, my lord."

"Aunt Mae! You're back!" I turned and saw my three precious daughters standing behind me. All of them had big smiles on their faces. Little Abigail was so excited she was hugging herself.

"Darling girls! Of course I wouldn't leave you!" Mama opened her arms wide and the girls rushed in, almost knocking me down in their haste. She looked up at me triumphantly.

Mama might have thought she'd won, but this was only a skirmish. I was determined to win the war.

# CHAPTER TWENTY-SEVEN

Dan was ridiculously happy at dinner that night. It was easy to tell that he thought all his troubles were behind him. Aunt Mae was back, the girls were elated, and I was doing my damnedest to put on a happy face,

"More pudding?" I asked sweetly, bringing the bowl to the table.

"You bet!" responded Dan enthusiastically. All three girls held their dessert bowls up for more as well. Mama made a show of refusing, but then reluctantly accepted seconds. I noticed it didn't take her long to slurp it up.

Later that night, I found myself dawdling over the dishes. Events had taken an interesting turn. Mama thought she could intimidate me, but it was quite obvious she needed me. She had no job, no money, and no committed relationship with her boyfriend. Whatever had really happened at Teddy's last night, the telling point was that she was back here.

With the kitchen finally cleaned to my standards, I joined my family and Mama in the den. They were all laughing over some silly sitcom on TV.

"Girls, you know there's no TV before homework is done. Get your backpacks and let's get busy."

Mama spoke up before they could move. "Oh, Jess, you're such a killjoy. Can't you ever relax and enjoy life? These little girls deserve a break every now and then."

I gave the girls "the look" without saying anything. They

jumped up and scurried for their schoolbooks. For good measure, I turned "the look" on Mama, too. I was pleased to see she averted her gaze.

"Sorry, honey, we just got sidetracked. I'll help Amelia with her math while you work with Amanda and Abigail." Dan scrambled up and headed for the dining room table.

I turned back to look at Mama as I left the room. She sat there pouting like a little child. I laughed to myself as I walked away. I was the one with the power now, and it was about time.

"Amanda, try again. Sound it out when you don't know it, don't just guess." I glanced impatiently at Abigail's worksheet, nodded my approval, and then sneaked a look at Dan and Amelia. They were working intently on her math—no tears, no anger, no anxiety. I sighed. Why couldn't Amelia see that I only had her best interests at heart? Why was she always fighting me?

I stood abruptly and picked up Amelia's backpack. "It's no wonder you're having trouble in school. Look at this backpack! It's stuffed full of papers in a complete mish-mash. Come over here and clean it out right now." I dumped the bag upside down on the table.

As Amelia slowly rose from her chair and came over to me, Dan shook his head. "Honey, we were just getting to the heart of fractions. Can't she do this later?"

"She's always going to do it later. No time like the present may be a cliché, but it's also true. Why did I bother buying you a notebook with pocket dividers if you're not going to use it?" I grabbed a handful of crumpled papers and started to smooth them out when something caught my attention.

In heavy black printing, on every line of the paper, this sentence was written: *Amelia is a bad girl.* Over and over again, like soldiers marching in a line. The printing was perfect. I looked at the other pages in my hand. They were identical.

Amelia gazed up at me with a pleading look in her eyes. She needed me! I folded the papers and tucked them under my arm.

"Maybe Daddy's right. This can wait until after you're finished with your math." I looked at her and gave a slight nod. She smiled back with just a hint of apprehension and took her seat beside her dad.

As I tried to focus on Amanda and Abigail's work, my thoughts were racing. Why would she have written such cruel words about herself? More to the point, why would she have saved them?

I wasn't able to speak with Amelia alone for another hour. Homework and bath time were over, the two little ones had been tucked in, and it was finally time for me to have a tête-à-tête with my eldest daughter.

Amelia finished her prayers as I stood over her. I suffered through "and please bless Auntie Mae" with commendable patience. When she was finally done, I bent over and patted her on the head.

"We have something to talk about," I said gravely. "Tell me about those papers."

Amelia scrunched down into her pillow as though she thought she could disappear. "I'll try to be a better girl, Mama—I promise."

I wrinkled my brow in bewilderment. "What do you mean? Yes, you're naughty sometimes—in fact, very naughty—but why do you think you're bad?"

She muttered something. "Speak up," I said impatiently. "You know how I hate it when you mumble."

"You think I'm bad," she said in a small voice.

"Amelia, I most certainly do not. You're a part of me, and I'm not bad, so how could you be? What are you talking about?"

She turned her head away from me and blinked back the tears that were starting to flow. "I'm sorry, Mama. I'll be good, I'll be really, really good. Please don't be mad."

"Are you trying to say that you didn't write those sentences?" I took a step back from her bed in consternation.

"You were just trying to help me, Mama. I know that."

A red haze glazed over my eyes. I couldn't believe she was accusing me of such juvenile behavior. Taking a deep breath, I finally spoke.

"Don't be ridiculous. I would never do such a thing. It was probably some classmate whom you offended. You've got to be more careful about how you treat people. Now go to sleep and forget all about it."

Amelia sneaked a glance at me. "Okay, Mama. Okay. I'm sorry." She pulled the blanket up under her chin and shut her eyes.

"Good night, then. We have a busy day tomorrow." I turned to walk out of her room, but something made me pause at the door. Amelia's eyes were wide open, and she was staring at me with a strange expression. It almost seemed to be one of vengeance.

# Chapter Twenty-Eight

After making sure the girls were all asleep, I told Dan that I needed to run to the store because we were out of toilet paper. He made a token fuss about going with me but I brushed him off. Of course I wasn't out of toilet paper—I never let us get low on the basics—I just needed some time to think. The grocery store was a soothing place to me.

Sure enough, when I found myself gliding down the aisles, gently pushing my cart as "Do You Know the Way to San Jose" played softly in the background, I could feel myself relax almost instantly. There was something about the grocery store that calmed me down. It was better than a spa day—I don't really like having people touch me, anyway. As I paused in front of a glistening display of apples, I thought back to the ugly words that someone had written about Amelia.

Who could have done such a thing? I moved on to the lettuce and a sudden thought invaded my serenity. Was it possible—was it at all possible—that Amelia had done it herself? Could she be devious enough to do such a thing? I nodded my head slowly. Yes, of course she could. I felt something squishy in my hand and looked down at a crushed tomato. I didn't even remember picking it up. I quickly threw it into a plastic bag along with two whole tomatoes. Of course I'd pay for it. That was the right thing to do.

I turned into the laundry aisle. The clean smell was intoxicating, and normally it was my favorite place in the entire store.

But something was bothering me, and it wasn't Amelia's silly game. I could deal with that. No, it was—it was—of course! Cousin Sally! I stopped in front of a shelf of dryer sheets, absentmindedly picking up a box and sniffing its lavender essence. Most of my dreams were of Mama's victims. Why, then, had I been remembering Cousin Sally? As far as I knew, she had not been harmed by Mama in any way.

I suddenly couldn't get out of the store fast enough. I needed to find out about Cousin Sally. Was there more to her story than I knew? I quickly paid for my purchases and drove home, thinking about how I could get the truth from Mama.

I walked in the front door and saw a light flickering from the family room. Pausing, I could hear Dan's deep rumbly voice and Mama's higher pitched squeal. I headed for the kitchen and put away my few purchases. Taking a deep breath, I walked into the family room.

"Hi, you two. What are you still doing up, babe? I thought you had surgery tomorrow." I looked at Dan with just a hint of reproach.

He sprang up from the couch. "Geez, you're right, as usual. Old man Hendricks is coming in for his root canal, bright and early. Guess I better get to bed. You coming, sweetie?"

I pretended to hesitate. "You know, I'm just not that tired yet. I think I'll stay down here and visit with Aunt Mae for a while." I smiled at the look of alarm that crossed Mama's face.

The look on Dan's face was priceless. "That's a great idea. Just what the two of you need—some time for girl talk." He winked broadly and headed upstairs.

I plopped down on the couch right next to Mama. "So, Mother dearest," I said in my sweetest voice, "I have a few things I'd like to talk over with you."

She leaned back into the arm of the couch as though she

were afraid I'd bite her. "I don't think we have anything to discuss. We both know the score."

"The score—hmmm, I'm not so sure about that. I thought it was Dolly three, victims zero—but now I'm thinking those numbers might be wrong." I tapped my index finger against my lips. "I'm wondering if there were some others who flew under the radar, so to speak. Maybe your parole officer would be interested in finding out."

Mama sat up straight, fairly bristling with indignation. "What the hell are you talkin' about, girl?" Her accent tended to creep in when she was under stress. "You don't have any business with my parole officer. And what kind of crap is this about victims? We both know the truth."

"The truth? The truth? Yes, we do, Mama." My voice was steely and determined. I wasn't going to let her weasel out of anything this time. "You killed my daddy, my stepdad, and my baby brother. Those are the ones they nailed you for. But I'm here to get at the *real* truth. I want to know just who else you got out of the way because they were inconvenient or they crossed you somehow. We're going to sit right here until I'm satisfied."

"You—you really don't know," Mama said, her eyes wide. "You really aren't right in the head."

I stood up, gasping for breath and clutching my chest. I felt like I was having a heart attack. Finally I forced out some words. "Don't you ever say that! Don't you ever say that again! I'm not crazy! I'm normal! I'm okay! Take it back—take it back!" I grabbed her by the arms and shook her.

Mama stood up, too. She calmly unlaced my fingers and held my hands in hers. "Darlin', you've been through a lot. Now, I have too, a' course. I'm the one who was locked up for all those years." She shuddered. "I don't know if I can ever make you see how awful that was. But you're right about one thing. It's time to set the record straight. Now let's sit down and act like regular people. Come on." She dropped my hands and patted the couch cushions. "Sit right here and let's talk."

Now I was the one pulling back, but I managed to sit down and take several deep breaths. When I could trust myself to speak, I said, "You say you suffered, but I did, too. I had to live in foster care—do you have any idea what that's like? And people were always looking at me, watching me, to see if I was a murderer like my mother. It's been hell, Mama—sheer hell."

Mama sat next to me, quiet and still. After a long moment she spoke. "Jess-girl, I want you to listen, just listen to me. Don't say anything until I'm done, okay?" She looked at me for confirmation that I got her message, and I nodded. She let out her breath in a deep gust.

"Here's the way it was. I was convicted of one death and one death only—little Nathan. They had a buncha' circumstantial crap about your daddy and Matt, but none of it stood up in court. But Nathan—well, doctors check for everything when a baby dies." Her face crumpled for a minute like she was about to cry, but she threw it off and went on. "He'd been given a shitload of alcohol, and it killed him. There was also some evidence that he'd been smothered." She stopped again, and looked me straight in the eyes. "We both know I wasn't home most of that night. You were the only one there."

I felt stiff and cold, like I'd been dumped in a deep freeze. My mind was working in slow motion, and I couldn't feel my body. It was strange, but not entirely unpleasant. It almost felt safe.

"Mama," I said, although it sounded like somebody else's voice, "there's no way you'd have been in prison for so long if it was just for Nathan. You're lying to me."

She shook her head. "Nope, they threw the book at me—added in as many other piddly charges as they could. My lawyer said it was because everybody thought I'd killed your daddy and Matt, and they were mad they couldn't prove it. So that's the truth, girl. I did one good thing in my life. I took the fall for you."

I tried to take in what she was saying, but I felt like I was slogging through mud. I remembered the night Nathan died. He'd been so fussy, and I had given him some whiskey—just like I'd seen Mama do. Had I given him too much? But I knew I hadn't smothered him—I loved him. I would never have hurt him on purpose, no matter how loudly he cried. I wouldn't, and I hadn't.

As we both sat there, the silence weighing heavy between us like a stone, I forced myself to put Nathan in the furthermost recess of my mind. I'd think about him later—mourn for him, remember him—but not now. Now I had to get the truth from Mama, while she was off guard and in a talking mood. I passed a hand over my eyes and then looked at her.

"Mama, I can't deal with that right now. I just can't. But I do have some questions for you. What can you tell me about my cousin Sally? And Grandma? I just have little wisps of memory about them. I need to know—are they all right? Are they alive?"

Mama continued to sit still as a statue. Finally she spoke. "Truth is, I don't know. That old beast you call 'Grandma' was never there for me. She hated me from the day I was born, and I returned the favor. I wouldn't have taken you to her house that time except I was desperate. 'Course, she didn't help us any—don't know why I thought she would. Now Sally—I'm not sure. I know my mother was takin' care of her for my brother Sam. He and his wife had split up and neither of them wanted to be bothered with a kid. Not like me—I was always there for you." She looked at me fiercely, daring me to contradict her. I was too tired to rise to the bait, so she continued.

"My mother always favored Sam over me. He could do no

wrong, and I could do nothin' right. Far as I know, he dumped Sally and took off without a fare-thee-well, but Mama always acted like he was the Lord himself. Why do you care anyway? You only met the two of them that one time." She looked at me in curiosity.

There was no way I was going to tell Mama about my dreams. She'd twist them into something crazy. "Oh, I don't know. Guess I thought it was strange that you never talked about them after we left Mississippi. And when you went to prison, the court thought there was no family around to take me in."

"They were right," Mama said bitterly. "I would never have let that old bitch get her hands on you. She would have poisoned your mind against me worse than it already was."

I stood up. Every bone in my body ached, and my mind still felt foggy with unresolved thoughts. "What say we call a truce, Mama? At least for now. I'm so tired I can't see straight. I've got to get to bed."

Mama stood up, too, but kept her distance. "Sure, darlin'. I understand. It's a lot to take in." She walked out of the family room, then paused at the doorway and turned. "I do love you, you know. You're a part of me—the best part." Then she headed off to her room.

I slowly made my way up the stairs. I wasn't a part of her—I wasn't. I didn't care what lies she told, I didn't even care about her parole officer. I needed to sleep, and please God, not to dream.

# CHAPTER TWENTY-NINE

*Sally and I were walking through a marshy meadow. "Watch out! You almost stepped in that cow pie!" She grabbed my arm and pulled me back.*

*"C-cow pie!" I giggled, and then we both broke into uncontrollable laughter.*

*Sally abruptly stopped laughing and looked at me sadly. "Jess, why doesn't your mama like me?"*

*"I dunno. Sometimes she acts one way and sometimes another. Let's not talk about her."*

*Then we turned around and we were suddenly in Grandma's kitchen. Grandma was at the sink with her back to the room. Mama was slouched in a kitchen chair, a discontented look on her face.*

*"You've never been there for me, Mama. You'd do anything for sweet baby Sam, even raise his brat while he goes out and has a good time, but nothing for me."*

*Grandma turned around and faced Mama. Neither of them seemed to notice that Sally and I were there.*

*"Sam didn't take our family name and drag it through the mud. Stealing, lying, sleeping around, spreading evil rumors—it didn't matter to you, you just picked up and left for California. But I have to live here, and face the townsfolk. You're nothing more than a common harlot. I don't know why you bothered to come back."*

*Mama looked mad enough to spit. She stood up, face to face with Grandma. Her hands were clenched in anger.*

*"You listen to me, you old hag. My husband died and left me*

*without a penny, or I wouldn't have come back. I don't know why I thought you'd have the common decency to help your daughter and grandchild. I should have known better. You never cared about me or took my side in anything. You always believed what other people had to say. Well, don't worry about us. We're going straight back to California on the next bus. I'll figure out something. My daughter deserves a good life. I have maternal instincts, not like you. But you better believe one thing—you'll be sorry for how you've treated us. You'll be damned sorry." She rushed out of the room, right by Sally and me, just as though we were invisible.*

*Sally took my hand. "It's okay, Jess. It's not your fault. My mama used to yell sometimes, too. Come on, let's go play."*

*I followed her out of the room, but something made me look back. Grandma's old black Buick was parked just outside the door, and Mama was standing by it with something in her hands, something shiny and metallic. I could hear a train whistle blowing mournfully in the distance.*

I woke up with a pounding headache. I couldn't remember my entire dream, but I knew it had been unpleasant. But there was no time to feel sorry for myself. My family depended on me; I set the tone for their days. If I was upbeat, efficient, and conscientious, they would be, too. Perhaps a brisk shower would shake off the lingering effects of my dream.

After showering and dressing, I went down to the kitchen. I wasn't quite in the mood for the mess of a big breakfast, so I decided on oatmeal—not the instant kind, that was no better than wallpaper paste. I was stirring the cereal when Mama walked in.

"Hello, darlin'," she said, somewhat hesitantly. "How was your night?"

I kept my attention on the oatmeal. "Fine. Yours?" Some scrap of memory was gnawing at my mind, but I couldn't seem to retrieve it.

"Oh, just wonderful. I dreamed about my dear Teddy. You know, we're going out tonight. He said he has something very special to talk over with me. I think he might be ready to pop the question!"

"Pop the—" I turned and looked at her. She sat there on the kitchen chair, all smug in her hot-pink negligee. Something about the way she was sitting brought back some of my dream, but they were just wispy fragments. "You mean, he wants to marry you?"

"Well, dear girl, I am a very attractive woman, and he is a man, with manly desires. I've made it very clear that he won't get the prize without a ring."

I winced. The prize indeed! It was a pretty shopworn trophy, in my opinion. Teddy seemed intelligent, but that didn't mean he could tell the difference between a silk purse and a sow's ear. On the other hand, Mama getting married would solve a lot of my problems. She'd be out of the house, and eventually I could ease her out of my life altogether.

"Well?" she questioned, her eyes flashing that brilliant green that always reminded me of ice-cold emeralds. "Aren't you happy for me? It'll get me out of your hair. Seems that alone would have you jumping for joy."

I hated how she could read my mind sometimes. "Of course, Mama, I'm very happy for you. But where would you be living? I thought you said Teddy's place was more of a bachelor pad— too crowded for the two of you."

"Oh, I have no doubt he'll get a more suitable place. He's got plenty of money, you know. Besides his government pension, he's made some very wise investments over the years. I do so love a man who knows how to handle finances." She smiled a cat-like smile.

We were interrupted by Dan and the kids coming in to see

what was taking so long with breakfast. "It's just oatmeal, I'm afraid. But we'll have a special dinner tonight to make up for it."

"Sweetie, oatmeal is just fine," Dan said, giving me a quick kiss. "Anything you make is delicious."

"I'll have to miss the feast tonight, I guess," Mama chimed in. "Teddy is taking me out, and he has something important to ask me." She blushed prettily.

My stomach turned over. "I thought you said he had something to talk over, not something to ask you," I said.

She waved her hands in the air. "Piffle, it's all in how you look at it. I prefer to focus on the bright side. You should try that sometime, Jess-girl. It makes life so much easier." With that parting shot she swept out of the room. "No breakfast for me, thanks. I'm saving up for tonight. Teddy always picks the best restaurants," she threw over her shoulder.

I bit my tongue and focused on dishing up the oatmeal with a smile on my face. With any luck, I'd really have something to smile about after Mama's date tonight.

# CHAPTER THIRTY

The day proceeded in an ordinary fashion. I basically sleep-walked through school—thank goodness I had established structure early in the year. The children knew that on certain days they had better be on their best behavior and follow the routine.

At last it was time to pick up the girls and go home. I was exhausted after my night of unpleasant dreams and was looking forward to an early evening. The girls scooted upstairs and put their things away. Normally they'd be asking for their after-school snacks, but they could see I was in no mood for nonsense.

Mama must have left with Teddy before we came home, because there was no sign of her. The only trace was the scent of her perfume when I walked past her room—she did tend to overdo on that. I could feel some of the tension draining out of me. At least I wouldn't have to contend with her tonight. I smiled to myself. Maybe she and Teddy would elope! No, I couldn't be that lucky.

Dinner was a quiet, calm affair. I had made the special meal I'd promised—fried chicken—and everyone seemed to appreciate it. Dan talked with the girls about school and friends and I basically just smiled and nodded. I couldn't wait to fall into bed.

As Dan was helping me clear the table, he stopped by the telephone. "What's this? The number for sub services? Aren't you feeling well? You didn't say anything."

I grabbed the crumpled paper out of his hand. "Oh, that's been there for weeks. I'm fine. I was at school today, and I'll be there tomorrow."

Dan looked at me strangely. Normally any stray papers were disposed of quickly in our house, but even I could miss something now and then.

"Never mind. I'll finish in here. You go and get the girls started on their homework." I kept the paper in my hand and turned toward the sink. "Go, go. I'm fine." A few seconds later I could hear him in the dining room with the girls. I breathed a sigh of relief and threw the paper into the garbage disposal.

With the kitchen cleaned and homework done, my family settled in to watch a little television. I looked at Dan and the girls and my heart swelled with pride. This was the way it was supposed to be—peaceful, orderly, harmonious. No hidden agendas, no evil masked as love. Amelia glanced away from the TV screen and smiled sweetly at me. Maybe it wasn't too late to redeem her, as long as Mama stayed out of our lives. I smiled back and leaned over and patted her head. Yes, everything was going to be all right after all.

"Okay, guys, bedtime," Dan said, getting up off the couch. "Who can get their teeth brushed first? One, two, three, go!"

I winced at his boisterous tone but I was relieved that he was taking over. I felt so tired that I couldn't even stand up. "I'll be up to say good night, honey-bunnies." I lifted my hand in a weak wave.

It was then that the phone rang. I looked at the clock—eight thirty. For some reason I knew it was important to check the time. I slowly dragged myself off the couch and picked up the phone.

"H-hello?"

"This is Sergeant Martin of the Roseville Police Department. May I speak with Mr. or Mrs. Stranahan, please?" The voice was cool and official.

"This is Mrs. Stranahan." My heart began to beat fast in my chest.

"Are you related to Mae LaRue?"

"Yes, she's my mo—I mean, my aunt. What's wrong? Has she been in an accident?" My voice must have risen, because the next thing I knew Dan was in the room.

"Honey, what's wrong? What's upsetting you?" I mutely handed the phone to him and sank back down on the couch.

"Who is—this is Dr. Stranahan, yes—what? Oh, I see. Um-hum. Okay. Of course. We'll be there right away. Thank you." He clicked off the phone and turned to me with a dazed look on his face,

"Well?" I said impatiently. "What is it? Is Aunt Mae okay? Is she hurt? What?"

He shook his head slowly. I didn't know if he meant "no" or if he was trying to clear his mind. He walked over and took my hands in his.

"Baby, you have to stay strong. Aunt Mae is okay—physically, at least. It's Teddy. He's . . . he's dead."

I burst into tears and threw myself into Dan's arms. "No, no, no! It's not fair! It's not right! It shouldn't have been him—it should have been her! No!"

"Honey, get hold of yourself! You don't know what you're saying! Shhh, shhh." He patted my hair like I was a child.

I drew back. "I'm sorry, Dan. I—I don't know what came over me. What happened? Was it an accident? A heart attack?"

Dan took a deep breath. "He drowned. Apparently they were out on his boat and he slipped and fell. I've got to go pick up Aunt Mae at the police station. They said she was hysterical when they got to the scene—they were almost ready to take her to the hospital—but she's calmed down now. Will you be okay while I'm gone? I could call Mary next door to watch the kids if you want to drive over with me."

I started to put my fake smile on, then realized it would be inappropriate. I arranged my face in a concerned look instead.

"I'll be fine. You go and get Aunt Mae. Poor thing, she must be a wreck. What a horrible experience." I gave him one last hug and ushered him out the door.

The minute I heard the car start up I began pacing up and down the living room. I was furious. I could imagine the scene Mama had put on for the police. They probably thought she was a poor distraught woman who had lost her true love. I knew better. I knew the real demon lurking behind those green eyes. Somehow I was going to make sure she paid for what she'd done.

I wasn't tired anymore. A fire was coursing through my veins, making it impossible to stay still. I needed to act, to do something, but I couldn't think clearly. "Slow down," I whispered to myself. "Slow down and use your brain."

As I stood still, taking deep breaths to calm my racing heart, a flash of inspiration struck. Of course! This was the perfect time to go through Mama's secret box. It would take Dan at least twenty minutes to get to the police station, so if I hurried I could go through all of the papers she'd stashed away. Maybe something in that box could help me figure out how to banish Mama from our lives once and for all.

# CHAPTER THIRTY-ONE

I rushed into Mama's room. The empty bird cage swung slightly on its stand as I opened the door. I shuddered. It was typical of Mama's morbid sentimentality that she would keep the cage up. She probably thought it would make me feel bad, but guilt could not exist when there had been no wrongdoing. I turned my back on the cage and got on my knees so I could reach the hidden box from underneath her bed.

It was gone. "Damn, damn, damn!" I swore out loud, a measure of my frustration. Where had she put it? More to the point, why had she moved it? I didn't think she'd noticed that I'd even touched the box, but something must have given me away.

No time to think of that now. I'd just have to be extra careful as I searched her room this time. I quickly got to work, checking the obvious places first—the closet, dresser drawers, even under her mattress. Nothing. I stood in the middle of the room, scanning for possible hiding places.

Of course—the guest bathroom. It was right next to Mama's room. She'd probably guessed that I'd check her room again. Her devious mind would work that way. I entered the bathroom and checked the cabinets and drawers. I was careful to keep everything in order, but it didn't matter. There was nothing to be found.

I left the bathroom just in time. I could see the car headlights illuminating the driveway. Dan and Mama were home, and I needed to prepare myself for the encounter. I smoothed my hair, took a deep breath, and went to the front door.

Dan entered with his arm around Mama. She was leaning against him like a wounded dove—or perhaps *soiled* dove would be more accurate. On second thought, dove was an inappropriate term for Mama in anyway. She was more like a raptor, seeking out her prey.

I pushed such images out of my head and approached the two of them. "Aunt Mae, I'm so sorry. You probably want to go straight to bed. We can talk in the morning."

She shook her head. "No, I'd like to talk about it now. I need to get it out. I—I don't think I could sleep tonight if I don't talk about it." She raised a tear-stained face to me. "Please, Jess, can't we just sit down together?"

Dan was looking at me pleadingly. I knew when I was beaten. "Of course, Aunt Mae. Sit right here on the couch. Can I get you something? Tea, water—or maybe a glass of whiskey? You have had a terrible shock, after all."

She gave me a sharp glance. She knew that whiskey might loosen her tongue a bit too much. "Thank you, dear girl. Just a glass of water will be fine. Oh—and could you put a bit of lemon in it? You know I have a hard time swallowing plain water."

I went to the kitchen, seething. She always had to have the last word. Well, we'd see what she had to say about poor Teddy. It didn't matter how she'd twist it, I knew that she was responsible for his death.

I came back into the living room and handed the glass to Mama. She was still huddled against Dan, and he was patting her shoulder. I steeled myself and sat on the other side of her, taking one of her hands in mine. "Why don't you try and calm down and tell us all about it," I said in a soothing tone.

She gulped some water and put the glass down on the coffee table. I winced when I saw she hadn't used a coaster, but I forced myself to ignore it.

"Well," she began in a trembling voice, "the night started off so wonderfully. Teddy prepared dinner for me on the boat. He's a gourmet cook, you know—I mean, *was*. Oh, I shall never get used to talking about him in the past tense! I just can't believe it!" Giant crocodile tears rolled down her cheeks.

Dan handed her his handkerchief, murmuring some "there there" nonsense. I stayed silent, waiting to hear her lies.

"Thank you, darlin'," she sniffed. "Anyway, we had some champagne during dinner. I guess we drank more than I realized. And he'd had a before-dinner drink, too, now that I think of it. Everything was just perfect, and then he said he wanted to get something from the top deck. He said it was a surprise for me. I just know it was my r-ring." She put her hands to her face and sobbed. I was unmoved. I'd heard that fake crying from her before many times in my childhood. If Mama couldn't bully her way with anger, she'd resort to tears. Dan, of course, was horrified.

"Let me get you a cold cloth for your eyes, Aunt Mae. You're going to make yourself sick." He jumped up from the couch and went into the bathroom.

When I could hear the water running, I spoke softly through clenched teeth. "You might have fooled Dan and the police—they're men, after all—but you don't fool me. I'm not buying this bull about a perfect night and a proposal. He was onto you, wasn't he? He found out about you somehow, and so you took care of him—in your own special way."

She dropped her hands and glared at me. Her voice was as low as mine. "I cannot believe you are so cruel. What have I done to deserve such hatefulness from you? Teddy loved me, and now he's gone. I deserve some sympathy, even from you."

Dan came back into the room then, clutching a damp washcloth in his hands. "Here you go, Aunt Mae. Just hold this up to your eyes. You know Teddy wouldn't have wanted to see you this way."

"Oh, Dan, you are so sweet and kind. Thank you so much. I do appreciate you." She took the cloth and dabbed at her eyes, shooting me a triumphant look under its cover. "It helps so much to know that you care."

"Of course, Aunt Mae. We both care, you know that." He sat down beside her again. "If you'd rather not go on talking about it, that's okay."

Mama took a deep breath and squared her shoulders. "No, I must be strong. It's what Teddy would have wanted. Well, I was sitting in the cabin, all excited because I just *knew* he was going to propose. And suddenly I heard a sort of shout, and then a splash—and then nothing. I was scared, I was so scared! I just knew something terrible had happened. We were too happy, and somehow I am never to have happiness in my life." She sighed dramatically. It was all I could do not to retch. She continued, reveling in an audience as usual.

"I sat there for a few seconds, frozen. But I knew I had to go out on deck and see what had happened. The wind had come up, and the boat was rocking, but I held onto the railing and called for him. There was no answer, nothing at all. And then I saw the water on the deck. He must have slipped and lost his footing somehow. The police said there was a—a head wound." She blinked back tears. "It was all over so fast."

Dan was transfixed by her story. "You poor little thing," he said, his voice breaking just a bit. "How did you get back to shore?"

She turned slightly toward him, wringing her hands. "Well, of course I wouldn't know the first thing about driving a boat." She giggled hysterically. "I guess you don't drive a boat, do you? But anyway, I remembered Teddy had shown me the radio before. I just got on it and said I needed help—that I was afraid there'd been an accident. Then these nice young Coast Guard men came, and the next thing I knew the police were there, and then you came, Dan, like my knight in shining armor." She gazed at him adoringly.

Oh, my God. This was her finest performance yet. Dan was eating up every crumb. I cleared my throat.

"I really think you should go to bed now, Aunt Mae. It's getting late. Just sleep in tomorrow. Maybe I should take the day off in case you need me." I stood up and took the washcloth and water glass from the table.

"Oh, no dear, please don't do that. I think I'll do better by myself. I have my memories to keep me company, you know."

I nodded and walked out of the room. I looked back and saw Dan slowly leading her to her bedroom as though she were an invalid. Her act had been a hit with him, but I knew better. I'd find out the truth about Teddy if it took every last ounce of my determination. She wouldn't get away with murder this time.

# CHAPTER THIRTY-TWO

I woke up the next morning to hear Dan talking on the telephone in a low voice. "Yes, I see," he said. "Does she need a lawyer? Can't you wait another day at least? She's exhausted." There was a pause, and then he said, "All right. Would two o'clock be okay? See you then."

He clicked off the phone, turned, and saw me staring at him. My face must have asked the question I did not speak, because he sat down beside me on the bed and took my hands in his.

"That was the police. They want to question Aunt Mae again. It's just routine, I'm sure. They probably always follow up after an unexpected death. People are too upset at the time to think straight. But just to be on the safe side, I'm going to call Rick. I don't think he's a criminal lawyer, but he can at least sit in on the conversation with her."

I nodded but stayed silent. I had a lot to do in a very short time, and I was trying to think where to start. A police investigation was going to spell trouble not only for Mama but for me. She had no ID in the name of Mae LaRue. If they dug a little too deep, all her secrets would be revealed—along with mine. I looked up at Dan. He had a concerned expression on his face and was gently rubbing my hands.

"Are you okay, sweetie? This is all such a shock, I know. Just remember, the police are only doing their job. Why, you've never even had a speeding ticket. It must seem like some sort of bizarro world to you." He managed a weak smile.

"You're right. It's not knowing what to expect that's so hard. Poor Aunt Mae, she's going to have a hard time with this. I doubt that she's had any more experience with the police than I have." It was amazing how the lies slipped off my tongue so easily. I resolutely closed the doors in my mind that held the many memories of dealing with the police.

I slipped my hands out of Dan's and got out of bed. "I'm staying home today. Aunt Mae will need us to be with her. Could you hand me the phone, please?"

He passed it over to me with a slight frown. "I've got to go into the office this morning for a couple of hours at least. After that I should be able to clear my afternoon appointments and come home. That way both of us can go in with her."

"Go in with her? You mean she has to be questioned at the police station? I thought they might come here." I was remembering the many times I had talked to police officers at my home as a child. The only time I was taken to the station was when Mama was finally arrested.

He shook his head. "No, they said they'd rather she came in. I'm sure it'll be no big deal—just a formality—but I'm going to call Rick. He owes me one, anyway. I gave him his last cleaning for free."

After calling in for a sub, I quickly showered and dressed. It was too early to wake the girls, but I had no compunctions about disturbing Mama. She got us both into this mess, so she'd have to help get us out.

I rapped lightly on her door. "Aunt Mae," I called softly. "We need to talk." She surprised me by opening the door immediately. She was still in her negligee, but her hair and makeup were fully done. Interesting. Whom had she been expecting—Dan? I was pretty sure she wasn't dolling herself up for me.

"May I come in? I think this is a conversation best had in private."

She didn't answer, just opened the door wide enough for me to slip in. She shut it after me. We stared at each other for a moment, then she waved me over to the bed. "Sit," she said tersely.

We sat side by side stiffly, not touching. I cleared my throat and began. "The police called this morning. They want you to come in today for further questioning."

"I expected as much," she said with a sigh. "Cops always want to poke, poke, poke until you tell 'em what they want to hear. What time?"

"I think Dan said two. The important thing is, how are we going to explain your lack of ID? We can't just say you're our dear sweet Aunt Mae and you somehow just didn't exist before you came to live with us. Maybe we can say you lost everything in a fire, and—"

Mama held up one hand. "Whoa, there, girl. I've got it covered." She reached for her purse and pulled out her wallet. When she flipped it open, I gasped. There was a Social Security card for "Marilyn LaRue." Behind it was a state ID card, and behind that a grocery store points card—all in the name of Marilyn LaRue.

"When did you have time to get all of these? And why do they say Marilyn instead of Mae?"

"Honestly, sometimes you don't have the sense God gave a billy goat. I knew I'd need ID when I got out. You can buy just about anything when you're inside. I wanted to start my new life as Marilyn, but you came up with that old lady-sounding 'Aunt Mae,' so I just went with it. We can tell the police that Mae is just a family nickname for Marilyn." She leaned back on the bed with a self-satisfied smirk.

I shook my head in mock disbelief. Nothing Mama did ever really surprised me anymore, but I just wanted to needle her a bit. "You really are the limit. Here you sit, so proud of yourself for being dishonest, when supposedly you're in mourning for your sweetheart. You'd better get your game face on before you talk to the police, or we'll all have hell to pay. I don't want to have to explain your sordid past to Dan and the girls, so get prepared to fake it like you never have before."

Mama sat up and wrapped her arms around herself. Her eyes filled up with tears. "Of course I'm mourning Teddy! He was a man among men. I was lucky to have him in my life even for just a little while. It wouldn't do any of us a bit of good if the police got all confused by my unfortunate life history. I just want this whole thing over and done with."

"For once we're on the same page. Make sure you dress in something with a little taste—I don't think the police are swayed by cleavage and clown makeup." I walked out and closed the door just in time to avoid being hit by the hairbrush Mama threw at me.

I went directly to Amelia's room. It was always hard to wake her. Sometimes I had the sneaking suspicion that she was already awake and just feigning sleep to torment me. I went into my usual routine.

"It's time to get up, it's time to get up, it's time to get up in the morning," I sang out, accompanying myself with energetic hand clapping.

Amelia groaned slightly but kept her eyes shut tight. I marched up to her bed and tore the covers off.

"No time for games today, little lady. I've got a busy day ahead of me, and I need you to get up and be a good example for your sisters. Out of bed right now."

She could tell by my tone of voice that it was futile to resist. I left her room once her feet were on the floor. I went on to Abigail and Amanda's room. They were probably already up, whispering and giggling to each other. Sometimes it was hard to believe that Amelia was their sister.

# CHAPTER THIRTY-THREE

I pulled away from the school parking lot with a sigh of relief. All three girls had moved at a snail's pace this morning, dawdling over their breakfasts, misplacing shoes, whining over hair combing. At least Mama hadn't made an appearance. I'd had about enough of her for one morning.

I decided to run a few errands before returning home. That would give me some more non-Mama time. If I worked it right, I'd get back shortly before Dan came home, and then he could provide a buffer. I turned into the shopping center and got out of the car.

I wandered through the aisles of Ross, idly picking items up and then replacing them on the shelves. Truth be told, there was nothing I really needed. I was just wasting time.

I found myself in the jewelry section. There, almost hidden among the gaudy glitz, was the perfect pair of earrings for Mama to wear for her interview. They were small tasteful pearls. Of course, since this was Ross, they weren't real, but they were near enough. I casually brushed against the jewelry display and opened my purse. They dropped in as smooth as spilled milk. I slowly sauntered around the perimeter of the store and walked out the door.

Once I was in the car I had to sit for a few minutes to calm my racing heart. What had I done? What was going on? This was behavior I had left far behind me, in my childhood. I pulled the earrings out of my purse, started the car, and threw them out the window. That sort of behavior must have been caused by stress—and, of course, stress was caused by Mama. No matter which way you looked at it, she was the root of all my troubles.

I checked my watch as I walked in the front door. Dan probably wouldn't be home for another hour. I could go to my room and close the door, or I could check in with Mama and make sure she was prepared for her interview. I braced myself and went to Mama's room. Doing the right thing might be hard, but that was no excuse.

Before I got to her door, it flew open so hard the doorknob hit the wall. Mama stood there, arms akimbo. "Well?" she said, twirling around. "What do you think?"

I gaped at her. She looked—well, she looked perfect. I couldn't have dressed her better myself. She wore tasteful slacks and a sweater set in a pale shade of blue. Instead of her usual ridiculously high heels, she had on a pair of bone-colored flats. Small gold posts were in her ears. The pearls would have really completed the look—but I wouldn't go there. I'd already forgotten about them.

"You look stunning," I said grudgingly. "You look like you belong to the country club set."

She beamed. That was one of her phrases: "country club set." She'd always aspired to be in that class.

"Thank you, dear heart. I appreciate those kind words. You see, your Mama is not such a bumpkin after all. I clean up pretty good, don't I?" Her face suddenly crumpled. "This is the way Teddy liked me to dress. Oh, if only he could see me now. What am I going to do without him?" She pulled a tissue out of her pocket and dabbed at her eyes, careful not to smear her mascara.

"Don't push it, Mama. Just try and be a little low-key. You don't want to draw any more attention to yourself than you already have."

She sniffed and raised her chin. "I was just going to get a bite to eat. Can I fix you something?"

I laughed out loud. "You fix me a meal? That's a laugh. How does soup and sandwiches sound?"

"Just fine, dear. Thank you for your kindness." Her sarcastic tone told me all I needed to know. She might dress up like a lady, but she was still the same old Mama.

We had just finished lunch and I was clearing the table when Dan came home. I hugged him before Mama could. "Can I get you something to eat, honey? It's no trouble."

"No, that's okay. I, uh—I picked something up on the way." His abashed tone meant that he'd been eating fast food again. It didn't matter how much I gently reminded him, he *would* continue to eat things that were clearly bad for him. I decided to let it go this time.

"Is Rick coming here or meeting us at the station?" I asked Dan.

Mama looked startled. "Now, who is this Rick again?" she questioned in a nervous tone.

"He's one of my golfing buddies, Aunt Mae. He's a good guy, and a cutthroat lawyer. He specializes in corporate law, but he agreed to sit in on this interview with you. He said it's probably just a formality. If he thinks you need more specialized help, he'll recommend someone good. He said he'll meet us at the station at two sharp, and one thing about Rick is, he's punctual." He patted her on the shoulder.

She reached up and clutched his hand. "Oh, Dan, you are so good to me. I don't know what I'd do if I had to face this all alone. I'd just be so frightened."

I decided it was time to put an end to this love fest. "It's a bit early, but maybe we should get going. There might be traffic, and I don't think it's a good idea to keep the police waiting."

"Right as usual, sweetie. Come on, Aunt Mae. We'll be with you all the way. You don't have a thing to worry about."

That's where you're wrong, I thought to myself as we headed out to Dan's Beemer. Mama has plenty to worry about—not from the police, but from me. I'd see to it justice was served in my own way.

# CHAPTER THIRTY-FOUR

Dan and I sat in the lobby of the police station on hard and remarkably ugly plastic chairs. Mama and Rick had been sequestered with a detective in one of the interview rooms for about half an hour. Rick was a large, hearty man, with a habit of clapping people on the back. He'd assured us that there was nothing to worry about.

I was nervous as a cat, wondering what Mama was saying in there. Could she convince them that she was Mae LaRue? Would she say something stupid that would give everything away? I was torn between wanting her to be punished for her depraved behavior and praying devoutly that she would get away with it. The problem was, if she were caught out in her lies, I would pay the price along with her. Dan would find out about my background, and even worse, he'd know that I had lied to him.

I was just glancing at my watch when the interview room door opened. Mama and Rick stood in the threshold and both shook hands with the detective. She must have pulled it off. I let out a deep sigh of relief. I hadn't realized I'd been holding my breath.

Dan and I stood up to meet them. Mama and Rick strode over to us, both fairly brimming with good spirits. I frowned slightly at Mama and shook my head. She was looking a bit too perky for someone who had lost her true love. She got my signal instantly and bent her head, dabbing at her eyes with a tissue.

She grabbed Rick's arm.

"Oh, you were so masterful in there! I couldn't have gone through that alone. Thank you so much." She looked up in his face adoringly.

"Now, now, it was nothing. It's pretty easy to defend an innocent party. I have to say, I almost enjoyed myself. Don't get much call to do this type of thing in my practice. Brought me back to my law school days. Apparently the poor guy slipped on a puddle of oil, not water. Easy to see how you could lose your footing. He must not have been much of a sailor, to have his boat in such poor condition." He reached out and shook Dan's hand. "So we're all fair and square now, m'man. You'd better get these two ladies home. The ambience here leaves something to be desired." He guffawed at his own joke.

Dan was the only one who talked much on the way home. "I hate to say we should celebrate, given the circumstances, but maybe we could do a little something in Teddy's honor. We could go to Romanini's tonight. What do you think?" He turned toward me.

"I suppose that would be all right. It's Friday, so there's no school tomorrow. It wouldn't be that disruptive to the girls' schedule."

Mama shuddered. "That's so very sweet of you, Dan, but I just don't think I'm up for it. I'd rather stay in tonight. But why don't you and Jess go out? You two need some time together. I could stay home with the girls. I'd love to do it."

"Out of the question!" I snapped. Dan looked at me in alarm as he turned into the after-school program's parking lot. I had made arrangements for the girls to stay there in case we were held up at the police station.

"Why not, Jess?" purred Mama. "I used to take care of you when you were little. I'm perfectly capable of watching such delightful creatures as your daughters."

"Maybe it would be too much for you, Aunt Mae. We could take the girls with us. Then you could get some rest."

"No, I insist," she said, leaning forward from the backseat. "Spending time with those precious girls would take my mind off"—her voice broke—"this whole horrible experience."

I sat with my mouth clamped shut. I knew if I dared to open it, I'd say something I would regret. Dan parked the car and looked from me to Mama and back again. "Well, Jess? What do you say?"

I felt trapped. I needed to keep Dan happy and believing in me, but the thought of Mama having unsupervised time with my children was anathema to me. "Let me go in and sign them out. I'll ask them how they'd feel about it." I opened the car door and hurried out.

As I entered the building, the first thing I noticed was Amelia sitting alone on a wooden chair near the doorway. She had her head down, her hair almost completely hiding her face.

"Amelia? What's the matter? Are you being punished? What did you do?"

She raised her head, glaring at me. "Why do you always think I've done something wrong? Maybe I just like to be by myself sometimes. Maybe I don't like to play with stupid babies all the time." She glanced scornfully to where her sisters were happily playing with a doll house.

I gritted my teeth. Just when I'd begun to soften toward her, she started up again with her defiant behavior. Instantaneously I made my decision about tonight. Mama could watch the girls and see how much fun it was. Dan and I would go out and pretend we were childless.

"Go get your sisters. I have to sign you out." I turned and walked to the front desk without looking back. She'd do as I said if she was smart.

Amanda and Abigail raced up to me with Amelia trailing

behind. "Mama, Mama! We had fun!" They were both squealing so loud, I wasn't sure which one was talking. I only knew it wasn't my eldest daughter.

As the door shut behind us, I knelt down so I could talk with my children on their level. "Girls, I need to talk to you about something. Mommy and Daddy are going out to dinner tonight. We won't be gone very long. Aunt Mae is going to stay home with you, and she'll expect you to follow my rules. Don't think you'll be able to put one over on her. I'm leaving her written instructions." I gave them a serious look.

Amanda nodded and spoke up first. "We'll be good, Mama. Will you bring us a doggy bag from the restaurant?"

"Yeah, or those little umbrellas from your grown-up drinks?" Abigail chimed in eagerly.

Amelia didn't speak, just stood there like a lump. There was a brief flicker of enthusiasm in her eyes, though. I hesitated for a moment. If she was excited about spending the evening with Mama, maybe I should reconsider. But by then, the two little girls had run to the car, shouting, "Aunt Mae! Aunt Mae! You get to babysit us!"

"I know, darlin's," said Mama as she made room for them in the backseat. "We're going to have such fun!"

"Mama said you had to follow her rules," said Amelia as she got into the car. "She said she's going to leave you instructions."

"Well, of course we'll do things your mama's way. If she says something is a no-no, then it's a no-no." Mama smiled in a phony way. I was pretty sure I saw her wink at Amelia. In any case, Amelia's face brightened considerably.

A wave of trepidation washed over me. Why had I let my impatience with Amelia get me into this situation? I should have trusted my first impulse. Giving Mama unfettered access to my girls was wrong, wrong, wrong. I turned to Dan to let him know I'd changed my mind, but he spoke first.

"Honey, I'm so glad we're doing this." He spoke so softly I had to strain to hear him over the babble of Mama and the girls chattering to each other. "I just feel like we haven't had much time together ever since—you know"—he nodded toward Mama—"I've missed you."

I sighed. "Me, too, honey, me, too." There was no way out. I'd just have to plan for damage control.

# CHAPTER THIRTY-FIVE

When we got home, Dan hurried to shower and change. I sat down at my desk and wrote out a list for Mama. When I was finished, I hunted for her and found her in the family room with the girls. They were all watching a nature documentary about whales.

"See, dear? We're just sitting here doing something educational." Mama gave me a dazzling smile. "We're going to have a nice, quiet evening."

I didn't acknowledge her remark. "Here's the list," I said, handing it over. "It covers bedtime, proper TV watching, and time-outs if necessary. There's a casserole in the freezer that I can defrost for dinner, and I've written down the instructions for heating it up. I've included my cell number, Dan's, and of course you know how to use nine-one-one." I stopped and looked at the four faces staring at me, mouths agape. You could certainly see the family resemblance. "Well? Any questions?"

Mama was the first to recover. "Sounds like you've thought of everything, as usual. Now scoot on upstairs and get ready. Don't worry about the casserole. I can certainly handle that."

I gave her a mistrustful look. "If you're sure . . ." My voice trailed off.

"Yes, yes. Now git, girl!" She made a shooing motion with her hands. The girls all sat demurely on the couch looking as though butter wouldn't melt in their mouths.

I turned and went upstairs, but my inner alarm was ringing

161

out of control. They were planning something, I just knew it. I'd have to outsmart them.

Twenty minutes later, Dan and I were ready to go. We had both dressed up a little, and Mama and the girls lavished praise on us.

"I just love the way that fabric drapes. And the color is perfect for you," Mama declared. I looked at her to see if she was joking—I was wearing black—but she seemed sincere.

As we walked through the door, I stopped to give one final directive. "Make sure you follow the list. We'll probably be late, so the girls should be in bed when we get home." Dan gave me a surprised smile. I had told him I thought we should make it an early night. He'd get over the disappointment. My plan was to pop back in unexpectedly. That way, I'd see what Mama was really up to.

I gazed at Dan over the candlelit dinner table. He was plowing into his manicotti with enthusiasm—almost too much enthusiasm, judging by the stain on his shirt. I pulled one of those instant-clean wipes from my purse and leaned over so I could reach him.

"Here, let me get that. If I blot it right now, the stain won't set. Honestly, sometimes I think you should tuck your napkin under your chin like some old farmer." I smiled to take the sting out of my words, but a brief expression of discontent flitted across his face. I stopped dabbing at his shirt and squeezed his hand. "I'm so glad we're doing this. Taking time for each other, I mean."

He smiled. "Me, too. Maybe after dinner we could stop at that jazz club on Fourth Street—you know the one, where we saw that guitarist from Jamaica."

"Heavens, Dan, that must have been five years ago at least! Your memory astounds me. And I'd love to but . . ." I let my voice trail off.

"You don't feel well," he intoned stonily. I guess I'd used that excuse once too often.

"No, I'm fine. I'm just concerned about Aunt Mae. I know she said she wanted to watch the girls tonight, but she *has* been through a tremendous ordeal, and I just don't want her to overdo."

Dan immediately looked guilty. "Man, I can be such a dope sometimes. Of course you're right. Here I was, just thinking of myself, and as usual you're more concerned with everybody else. Maybe later, after all this is behind her, we could ask Aunt Mae to sit with the girls again and make more of a night of it."

"That's a great idea, honey. I think that's our waiter, if you could just give him a nod. Don't forget to ask for doggie bags. The girls are expecting them."

Dan and I chatted inconsequentially on the drive home. I did my best to act relaxed, but inside I was tense as a freshman on the first day of high school. I was trying to mentally prepare for the confrontation with Mama when we got home—for confrontation there would surely be. There was no way she would have followed my rules if she thought she could get away with it.

We pulled into the driveway. The porch light was on, and a living room light, but other than that the house was dark. Probably has them all huddled up by the TV in the dark, spilling popcorn and soda everywhere, I thought to myself.

As we entered, I strained to hear the TV, or giggling, or *something,* but the house was quiet. I rushed into the family room. Mama sat there alone, watching an old black and white movie with the sound turned low. A little blond girl with braids was saying something and smiling in a disturbing way. An ominous feeling washed over me, but I shrugged it off.

"Hello, baby girl. Did you have a nice time? Why are you home so early? I thought you were going to make a night of it,"

Mama said, turning from the TV.

"I—I, uh," I stammered. Dan came in and rescued me. He put his arm around me.

"That was my idea, Aunt Mae, but you know this niece of yours. She's always thinking of others. She reminded me that you've had a pretty rough time of it and maybe we should come home and give you a break. How were the girls?"

"Just darlin'. I don't know when I've known more precious girls, except this one here." She rose from the couch and gave me a hug. I recoiled only slightly. "We followed all your rules to the letter." She pulled my list out of her pocket and waved it triumphantly in my face.

I grabbed the piece of paper. "Thank you so much, Aunt Mae. I'm just going to go up and tuck the girls in now."

"Do you really think that's a good idea? I mean, you don't want to disrupt their sleep. I've heard that can be very damaging to children." She fluttered her hands anxiously.

Here we go, I thought. There was something she didn't want me to know. I turned and charged up the stairs. Better hit Amelia's room first; she'd be the most likely partner in crime for Mama.

I walked silently into the bedroom. Amelia appeared to be sound asleep, but something struck me as out of the ordinary as I neared her bed. It was a smell, a distinct smell of—pizza! I whipped off the covers and turned on the light.

"All right, young lady. Tell me everything that happened tonight, and I do mean everything."

Amelia sat up and rubbed her eyes. I wasn't buying that she had been asleep, though. She fake woke up much too easily.

"I don't know what you're talking about, Mama," she mumbled. I grabbed her by the chin.

"Oh, no? Then what's that on your lips? Lipstick? And what about the smell of pizza? What happened to my casserole? And you've got your shorts on under your nightgown! What went on here tonight?"

Before she could answer, Dan and Mama burst into the room behind me. "Jess, it's okay. Aunt Mae explained everything. Calm down, honey." Mama wisely said nothing.

"I just bet she did," I snarled. "She always has an explanation for everything. But she deliberately flouted my rules and tried to undermine my authority. How does she explain that?"

"Let's go out in the hall and discuss this. No need for Amelia to lose sleep over it." Mama gestured for me to follow her out of the room. Still seething, I did.

"Well?" I said, my arms folded tightly in front of me. It seemed the only way I could stop myself from slapping her right across her smug little face. Dan put both hands on my shoulder as if he knew he needed to help hold me back.

"Jess, the truth is I was feeling lonely and sad tonight. I kept the girls up and played silly games with them to keep myself from sinking into despair. I didn't mean to upset you—that was the furthest thing from my mind." Mama looked at me with clear, guilt-free eyes. How did she do that, when the exact opposite was true?

"And I guess you didn't intend to look like the 'fun one' while I came off as the wicked witch, right?"

"Of course not! I was just having such a good time with the girls, and not thinking about Teddy, that things just got out of hand. I'll understand if you don't want me to sit with them again."

"Oh, never mind. It's not worth trying to explain anything to you. I'm going to bed." I turned and walked into my room, but stood just inside the door until I saw that both Mama and Dan had gone downstairs. I crept into Amelia's room without turning on the light.

She appeared to be really asleep this time; no wonder, since it was way past her bedtime. I moved stealthily toward her desk. I wanted to check her backpack. She'd never mentioned a word about her missing journal, but I'd bet money that she had started another one. I'd finally finished her old one. There wasn't much more to it than I'd read that first day. She'd obviously just started it.

There it was, tucked inside her school binder. I picked it up, glanced over to make sure she was asleep, and opened it. She might have written in it while Dan and I were out, something about how much fun she had with Aunt Mae and how boring I was.

She must not have had time to write in it tonight, but there was something else in the journal—something that made me lose my breath and feel faint. Taped to one of the pages was a yellow feather. Next to it were written these words: *Now she'll like me best again.*

# CHAPTER THIRTY-SIX

I stared at the journal and then shakily replaced it in the backpack. I slowly walked back to my room. I could hear Dan coming up the stairs, so I quickly threw off my clothes, put on my nightgown, and got under the covers. Amelia wasn't the only one who could fake sleep. I kept my eyes shut and slowed my breathing as he entered the room. Before long I felt the bed give as he lay down. It wasn't long until he was gently snoring.

I knew I wouldn't be sleeping that night. I could no longer pretend that Amelia was simply a willful child. She was worse than that, much worse. She had Mama's blood in her. Somehow the evil had passed over me, but it was in Amelia with a vengeance. I thought I'd been so careful, raising her the way I wished I'd been raised. I was always there before and after school, I made nutritious meals, I supported her in all of her activities. No one would ever tease her about her discount store shoes or clothes.

And she certainly had never been exposed to violence or drunken arguments. She'd never had to worry about the police grabbing her when she was on the way out of a store, or not be sure where she was going to sleep at night. No, Amelia had definitely had all the advantages that had dangled just out of my reach as a young girl. Television and the movies showed me what it was like to live in a pretty house on a pretty street, with pretty people. People who spoke in calm voices, people who were reliable and stable. I vowed that I would provide that type of life for my own children someday, and I did.

So if I had done everything right, then the fault was in Amelia. More precisely, the fault was in Mama. She was the one who was deep-down evil. Maybe it had started with her own mother or grandmother—I didn't know and I didn't care. All I knew was the hell I had lived in because of her. And now my own daughter was threatening to engulf me in a whole new nightmare.

It all reminded me of something I'd learned in college. We studied mythology in one of my literature classes, and the story of the Gordian knot especially interested me. The knot had been tied by an ancient king, and no one could untie it. Only Alexander the Great was able to figure out the simple solution. He cut it with his sword. My life with Mama—and now Amelia—was tied up in theirs like that knot. Unhappily for me, there was no hero in the wings waiting to solve this tangled mess.

I pressed my thumbs against my temples, trying to push back the headache that was trying to break through. That yellow feather. It could only mean one thing. Amelia had destroyed the bird because Mama was showing it love and attention. She couldn't stand to be second-best. It was horrible enough that Amelia had actually taken the life of an innocent (albeit dirty and obnoxious) creature. What made it even worse was that she did it out of a need for Mama's affection, not mine. I sacrificed for her, cared for her, nurtured her, but that all meant nothing. It was Mama with her fancy ways and silly talk that struck a chord with Amelia.

I sat up and pushed my feet into my slippers. Grabbing my robe and putting it on, I quietly walked out of the bedroom. Maybe some warm milk would help me to relax and get at least a little sleep. As I stepped into the hallway, I heard a voice. "Mama," it wailed.

It wasn't Amelia; it was coming from the little ones' room. I hurried down the hall and opened their door. Amanda was sitting up in bed crying. Abigail, bless her, was sleeping soundly.

"Mama, I threw up," Amanda sniffed through her tears. Sure enough, there were globs of vomit on her quilt.

"Shh now, you'll wake your sister. Did you have pizza and soda while Daddy and I were gone?" I stripped her quilt off the bed and bundled it on the floor, then picked her up and headed for the bathroom.

"Uh-huh," she replied, leaning her head against my neck. "I had three pieces."

"Maybe now you'll know why I don't like you to eat such greasy things. They're hard to digest. And too much soda is very bad for you." I sat her down on the closed toilet seat and wiped her face, then filled a cup with water. "Swish this around in your mouth and then spit it in the sink. Then it's back to bed with you."

She did as I instructed, then gave me a big hug. "I'm sorry, Mama. I won't ever do that again. I'll always listen to you."

I felt a warm glow spread through my entire body. She understood! She knew that I only had her best interests at heart, because experience had proven that to her. I returned the hug and then carried her back to bed. She was really too big to be carried, but sometimes I just couldn't resist.

I tucked her in with a clean quilt, kissed her, and then took the soiled quilt downstairs to the laundry room. I rinsed it out in the laundry tub but decided not to put it in the washing machine. Sometimes the washer made a thumping noise, and the laundry room shared a wall with Mama's room. The last thing I needed was to have her pop her head out wondering what was disturbing her beauty sleep.

I walked into the kitchen. As long as I was downstairs, I might as well make that warm milk. I wasn't sure I really needed it now that I'd been relaxed by Amanda's words, but it couldn't hurt. I poured some milk into a saucepan and sat down to wait for it to heat up.

How could sisters be so different? I treated them all the same, I was sure of it. Dan sometimes thought I expected more out of Amelia than the other two, but that was only natural. She was the oldest, so of course I depended on her to be a good example to her sisters. I remembered spending hours with her when she was in kindergarten, having her rewrite her name over and over. I knew she was capable of doing excellent work, so I sat with her until she produced it.

I thought she'd be proud of herself when her teacher put her paper on the wall with a big star by her name, but she only shrugged her shoulders when I tried to congratulate her. "See?" I'd said, "Mommy was right to have you practice. Now your teacher knows what a good student you are." She'd just stared at me without expression.

It was the same with her piano lessons. I had longed to take music lessons when I was a girl, so of course I provided them for Amelia. She never showed any gratitude at all. I would stand over her for the full hour of her practice time and keep the beat for her by clapping my hands together. Her teacher didn't believe in using a metronome, so I made do. And it worked—she was progressing very nicely in her musical education.

I got up and poured the scalded milk into a mug. As I stood there sipping it, I came to a decision. I could not let my daughter succumb to her lower nature. After all, she was *my* child. That meant that she had absorbed decency and respectability from me. I would not give up on her. It would mean increasing my vigilance, but after all, wasn't that a mother's job? I rinsed the mug, spoon, and pan and placed them in the dishwasher. Then, just for good measure, I wiped the counter down with an antibacterial cleaner. It was always best to finish a job completely.

# CHAPTER THIRTY-SEVEN

After a few fitful hours of sleep, I finally gave up and decided to get an early start on my Saturday. I threw some dish towels into the washing machine along with Amanda's quilt. I admit, I took a bit of perverse pleasure in starting the wash early in the morning. If I couldn't sleep, why should Mama?

Sure enough, she came stumbling into the kitchen just as I'd started mixing my orange muffins. She was bleary-eyed and her hair was a mess.

"What is that gawd-awful noise? My head is throbbing." She daintily put a hand to her forehead.

"It's called a 'washing machine,' " I enunciated in an exaggerated way. "It's used for cleaning clothes for a family." I put on a mock look of surprise. "Oh, I forgot. You wouldn't know about things like that. I did all the laundry for you. I always wondered—who did it before I was old enough to reach the controls? It must have been Daddy, but I don't remember him ever going near the washer. I guess you convinced him it was my job, not his."

Mama looked at me with loathing. "Your darling daddy never went near the washer—or the vacuum, or the kitchen sink. He expected me to wait on him hand and foot, even when I was pregnant with you. It was all too much for my delicate nature. I thought you liked doing little jobs for me. I always told people you were Mama's little helper. Now I see you're using that against me, too. I swear, you'd complain if Jesus himself came down and gave you a five dollar bill. There's no pleasing you—never was, never will be."

We were standing nose to nose, glaring at each other. I was so angry it took me a minute to see Amelia standing in the doorway. She didn't look shocked or upset; she just stood there with a slight smile on her face.

"Amelia! I—uh, Aunt Mae and I were just having a little disagreement. It's nothing, really, just some silly difference of opinion. I thought I was right, and she thought . . ." My voice trailed off as I realized I was babbling. I looked at Mama. She stood there with her arms folded across her chest and a smirk on her face.

"She knows," she said succinctly.

"Knows what? I don't know what you're talking about. Amelia, has Aunt Mae been telling you stories? Sometimes she likes to make things up, just for fun."

Amelia looked at me coolly. "She's your real mother, isn't she? I sort of guessed, but then *she* told me the truth. *She* knew I was old enough to understand."

I looked wildly from Mama to Amelia. "It's not true. My mother was a wonderful woman who was killed tragically in a car accident. She and my father loved me very much. They wanted only the best for me, but they were taken too soon. My real mother was cultured and genteel, a lovely person. She taught me how to be a good mother myself."

Mama shook her head sadly. "I can't believe you would disrespect me in this way. Imagine, making up a mama when you have a perfectly good one right here in front of you. Now Amelia knows all about why we were parted for so many years. I told her about the nasty divorce, and your daddy taking off and hiding you from me. Why, I searched and searched for you, but it wasn't until the internet got invented—by that nice southern boy Mr. Gore, I do believe—that I was able to find you. And it's been just wonderful being reunited, hasn't it, dear girl?"

I was ready to open my mouth and shout the truth, but Mama shot me a warning glance. There was something more behind this story, and until I knew what it was, I figured it was better to play along.

"Yes, Amelia, I guess you are old enough to understand. Sometimes grownups do strange things. I grew up being told my mother was dead to me, so it was just easier to tell people she really did die in an accident. I was sort of embarrassed for people to find out what really happened. You forgive me for not being entirely honest, don't you? Aunt Mae—I mean, Grandma—and I both agreed to keep the secret." I held out my hands to her.

Amelia took a few slow, deliberate steps toward me and clasped my hands. "I forgive you, Mama. And don't worry. Grandma told me to keep it all to myself. I won't tell Daddy or Amanda and Abigail. You can do that when you're ready. I'm real good at keeping secrets."

I shuddered a little when she said that. She certainly was. Her secrets were dark and twisted, not the innocent little stories of a young girl. It was my job to root out that darkness and return her to her true nature. I wasn't sure how to go about it, but the first step would surely be to repair our relationship. I needed to win her back from Mama.

"You're being very mature about this, Amelia. I suppose I didn't appreciate how grown up you've become. Maybe we can start doing some mother-daughter things together. Would you like that?"

She shrugged. "I guess. What about Grandma? She's your mom. Can she do things with us, too?"

The gloating look on Mama's face turned my stomach. I turned my attention back to Amelia.

"We'll see. But you have to be careful about calling her Grandma. For now, she's still Aunt Mae. Understand?"

She nodded and turned to leave the kitchen. "I'm going to go watch TV. There's a new episode of *Austin and Ally* on. I'll do my chores after it's over."

I stood there with my mouth open. Was she blackmailing me? She knew that I never allowed TV before Saturday chores. Maybe I was being too harsh on her. She was probably just reacting to our new, more positive relationship. Of course that was it. I believed that for all of two seconds until Mama let loose with an obnoxious giggle.

"She's got you right where she wants you, Jess-girl. You better stay on your toes if you know what's good for you."

"Oh, oh just be quiet! I've got muffins to make." My muffins! They were ruined. The batter had been sitting getting sticky while we'd been talking. Now I was going to have to start all over again. I began scraping the contents of the bowl into the sink.

"Since I'm up so early, I think I'll give myself a manicure. Call me when breakfast is ready. Ta-ta." Mama swept out of the room like a queen departing her court. I waited until I heard her door shut before I threw my mixing spoon in her direction. It made a mess but it was worth it.

# Chapter Thirty-Eight

We were just finishing breakfast—the muffins were a big success—when Mama leaned over her plate, head in hand. "I have such a heavy load on my mind," she said dramatically. "I just don't know what to do."

"What is it, Aunt Mae? Can we help?" Dan had his eager puppy look on his face. "You know you don't have to bear your burdens alone."

I nodded to the girls, excusing them from the table. Amelia looked like she wanted to linger, but I gave her a stern look and she reluctantly left the room. I didn't want the children around to hear whatever outlandish thing Mama was going to spring on us.

"Well, you see, I've been fretting about Teddy and his last wishes." She dabbed at her eyes with her napkin. "I know it might sound morbid to you young folk, but he and I had some serious talks about—well, you know." She looked appealingly at Dan.

He was clueless. "About what? I'm not sure I'm following you."

I decided to rescue him. "She means that they talked about funerals and wills. Isn't that right, Aunt Mae?"

"That sounds so crass when you put it that way, but yes, that is what I was trying to say." She shot me a venomous glance, then turned to Dan all dewy-eyed. "He told me that he wanted to be cremated and have his ashes tossed into the ocean. Teddy didn't have any children, and he'd been divorced for years. So what I've been wondering is, how can I make sure his plans are honored? I don't know who to contact or what to do first."

"I think we should call Rick. He can do a little digging for us, find out who Teddy's attorney was, that sort of thing. Then we'll know how to proceed." Dan patted Mama's outstretched hands. "Don't you worry. We'll do right by Teddy." He looked at his watch. "Hey, I better get going if I want to make my tee time. I'm actually playing with Rick today, so I can pick his brain on the nineteenth hole." He chuckled.

"Thank you so much, dear heart. You are just the best so—I mean nephew—anyone could ask for." She all but fluttered her eyelashes.

As soon as he left the room, I couldn't contain myself any longer. "Honestly, Mama. You are so transparent. Worried about Teddy's last wishes, my eye. More like you're worried about what will happen to his estate. You might as well simmer down, because I doubt very seriously that Teddy changed his will in your favor after such a brief relationship. Get real." I started clearing the table.

Mama stood up and flung her head back. "That shows how much you know. Teddy and I were soul mates. He understood the real me. He said he'd never met a woman like me in his whole life." Her eyes were sending out sparks as she lowered her head and glared at me.

I snorted. "I'm sure he'd never met anyone like you, but as far as knowing the real you, I don't think so—unless he did a background check."

Mama blinked when I said that, then turned and swept out of the room. I knew it! Teddy was ex-FBI, after all. If he was getting serious about someone, it made sense that he would investigate her past. At the very least, it would have come out that Mama was not who she said she was. The local police might have been fooled by her fake ID, but Teddy was a more formidable adversary. And the fact that he died so suddenly only confirmed my suspicions. His "accident" was no accident.

I was scrubbing out the kitchen sink when Amelia wandered in. "So Mama, could we do something special today? Just you, me and Gr—I mean, Aunt Mae? You said we would." She stared at me accusingly, daring me to say no.

I winced inwardly. Saturdays were such busy days for me. There was laundry to catch up on, cleaning, yard work. I'd been planning on washing the downstairs windows today. And of course, spending quality time with Mama was pretty low on my list of priorities. On the other hand, I needed to start winning Amelia over to my side. I sighed. My decision was made.

"That's a great idea, honey," I said brightly. "Let me think for a bit. We could go to the park, or a movie, or—I've got it! Let's have lunch at that little tea shop downtown! I bet your sisters would love to come, too."

Amelia's face turned stormy. "No, they're too little. You said you were going to do special things with me because I'm more mature. You always lie!"

I couldn't stop myself. I slapped her right across the face. She took a step back, too shocked to cry. Instead, tears came to my eyes.

"I'm so sorry, baby! Please forgive me! I've just been so upset. I didn't know what I was doing." I got on my knees and threw my arms around her.

She stood there stiffly, not returning my embrace. I pulled back and looked at her. "You do understand, don't you? I wasn't myself. I would never do something like that normally. There's just been so much confusion and stress in our home ever since—"

"Ever since what? Ever since I showed up? What have you been doing to this child?" Mama suddenly appeared behind

Amelia. She put her hands on my daughter's shoulders. Amelia leaned into her and away from me.

I put my hands on my stomach and took a deep breath as I stood up. "I won't pretend. It has been rough having you here, showing up out of the blue. I've done my best to keep things running in our usual routine, but it's been exhausting. I had a momentary lapse, but it's over now. Amelia understands. She's all right."

"Are you all right, Amelia? You can tell me." Mama spoke protectively.

She took her time answering, knowing that she had both of our undivided attention. She looked from Mama to me, and then finally spoke.

"I think if we all three go to the tea shop for lunch, we'll feel better. I'm going to go get ready." She pulled away from Mama, to my delight, and ran upstairs.

"Well, Jess? Are you up for it? A civilized luncheon with your two favorite females?" sneered Mama, her hands on her hips.

"Of course, Mama. I've taught myself to rise to any occasion. I'm sure we'll have a lovely time." I smiled regally and brushed past her as I left the kitchen.

I may have made the perfect exit, but inside my heart was pounding. It frightened me that I had lost control in such a low-class manner. I had always prided myself on never having to resort to physical punishment with my children. I taught them the right way to behave and usually all it took was a disappointed look from me to get them back on track. They wanted to please me. Amelia and Mama combined had thrown me off balance. I was going to have to muster all of my inner strength to overcome them.

After I'd arranged for a sitter, showered, and changed, I felt more composed. When I came downstairs, Mama and Amelia were sitting on the living room couch waiting for me. They would have been comical if they weren't so grotesque. Mama was wearing a huge sunhat with bright yellow roses on it, yellow gloves, and a low-cut ruffled dress that might have been appropriate on someone thirty years younger. Amelia was wearing her last year's Easter dress that was too short and too tight. She loved the dress so much that she had stubbornly refused to pass it down to Amanda. As I got closer I saw that she had lipstick on. Stay calm, I told myself. Act like you don't notice a thing.

"Gosh, Mama, you didn't hardly dress up at all," Amelia said with disappointment. Mama nodded in agreement.

I looked down at my white eyelet blouse, floral skirt, and ballet flats. This was definitely dressier than my usual daily attire. The difference was I knew what was in good taste and they didn't. So be it.

"We can leave as soon as Suzy gets here. She's going to sit with the girls until Daddy gets home from golfing. Oh, that must be her now." I opened the front door and let in the neighbor girl. Her eyes widened when she saw how Mama and Amelia were dressed, but she wisely said nothing.

After a few quick instructions to the sitter the three of us got in the car for our "mother-daughter" outing. If I could survive this without losing my composure, I could get through anything.

# CHAPTER THIRTY-NINE

As we drove toward the tea shop, I kept my eyes on the road but my ears tuned in to Mama's and Amelia's conversation. They were chattering as if they were contemporaries. I couldn't decide if Mama was extremely childish or if Amelia was artificially mature. I spotted our destination on the right and turned in.

"Here we are, girls," I said brightly. "This should be fun." I was determined to make it that way, come hell or high water.

"Oh, look how sweet!" exclaimed Mama. "It looks just like a doll house."

"I lo-o-ve it!" squealed Amelia. "Look at the cute little walkway! It's clobber stone."

"Cobblestone," I said automatically, then wished I hadn't. My daughter's face fell at my correction. I was going to have to watch what I said if we were going to develop the close-knit relationship I had in mind.

A silvery bell announced us as we entered the brightly painted door. A woman dressed in some sort of a fairy godmother outfit pranced in from the back of the shop. Her full-length dress was pink satin trimmed with silver lace. She held a glittery wand and waved it at us as she smiled in greeting.

"Hello, hello. Welcome to The Princess and the Tea. I am Celestina Luna, the guardian of your sojourn to this magical experience. It is so lovely to have you here. And oh, my dear, I adore your hat!" She smiled at Mama. Her voice trilled annoyingly, similar to that of Glinda the Good Witch. I could feel a tension headache starting behind my eyes. This could prove to be a very long afternoon.

Mama and Amelia were giddy with delight. They rushed around, oohing and aahing over all the little tchotchkes that were scattered around the foyer. There were fairies, rainbows, flowers, and castles. Everywhere I looked my eyes were assaulted with garish excess. I had envisioned a sedate English tea shop, not this wild mish-mash of tackiness. But my daughter was thrilled with it, so I needed to at least pretend to be enthusiastic.

"This is an adorable place. You've really gone all out with your theme," I said in as warm a tone as I could manage. "Everything is so—so—magical," I finished lamely.

Luckily she accepted the comment without question. "Thank you so much, my dear. Now let me show you to your own special tea room. Every party gets a private space. It just adds so much to your enchanting experience. And let me guess—do we have three generations here?" Her glossy pink lips turned up in a wide smile.

"You are clairvoyant!" Mama laughed. "Yes, this is my daughter Jess, my granddaughter Amelia, and I'm Dolly." She held out her yellow-gloved hand. Celestina Luna immediately shook it, then dropped in a curtsey.

I noticed Amelia start when Mama introduced herself as Dolly, but the curtsey apparently whisked all questions out of her mind. When the proprietress turned and did the same to Amelia and then me, I thought I was going to have to pick my daughter up off the floor.

"Oh, thank you," she said breathlessly, her eyes glittering with excitement.

"No, thank *you* for coming to my humble shop. And now, ladies, let me take you to your magic chamber." She whisked us into a room off to the left.

Before we crossed the threshold, she picked up a hatbox from a rickety-looking table outside the door. "Here is your crowning touch! This wouldn't be a special tea without *tea*-aras! Get it? Tiaras, tea-aras? It's funnier in print."

Mama and Amelia laughed unreservedly at the lame pun. I managed to utter a few ha-has. We all put on the tiaras and entered our room. It was more of the same—little figurines on little tables, murals on the walls, and fairies, fairies everywhere. The tablecloth was a vintage floral print. I looked dubiously at the chairs. They seemed a bit wobbly, but I decided to keep quiet. I was going to prove to Amelia that I could enjoy doing things with her.

Reading the menu took some time. Mama and Amelia kept stopping to exclaim over the "darling" items on the menu— sugar cookies sprinkled with pixie dust, for example, and fairy cakes with enchanted icing. We eventually got through it and placed our orders. Once we were alone, I smiled brightly and decided to offer an olive branch.

"I must say, you two fit in here much better than I do. Your outfits are perfect for a fairy tea room. I feel underdressed."

Mama smiled back, just as phonily. "Well, Jess, you've always been one for hiding your light under a bushel. Thank goodness Amelia takes after me. She knows how to stand out in a crowd."

For a minute I was completely flummoxed. Amelia stand out? She usually acted like she was trying to fade into the woodwork. She'd deliberately cover her face with her hair to block people out. But looking at her today, I saw a different girl. She was sitting up straight, happy, with her hair tied back with a white ribbon. Even the too-small dress was flattering in this setting. What had caused this change? Could it have been Mama's influence?

Just then Celestina Luna came warbling in with a large silver tray. She went on about our magical meals and the fairy-tested way of pouring tea. I barely heard her. Mama's words burned in my brain—"Thank goodness Amelia takes after me." It wasn't fair that Mama was trying to take over my daughter. Amelia wasn't like Mama, she wasn't. I looked across the table at the two of them as our fairy godwaitress finally left the room.

"So Amelia, I suppose you're wondering why your grandmother introduced herself as Dolly." I kept an innocent look on my face.

Amelia took a sip of her tea, wrinkled her nose, and added more sugar before she replied. "Yeah, that was sort of weird. I thought your name was Mae, Grandma. Do you have a secret identity?" She laughed.

"It's just a nickname, honey. I have several—Mae, Dolly, Marilyn. Sometimes it's fun to choose a different name, depending on how you feel. What name would you pick for yourself today, right this very minute?"

"Cool! I think I'd like to be called Anastasia Seraphina—wait, no, Sophia Sylvia. And you could call me Sophie for short. I love that name."

"Don't be ridiculous," I cut in. "You have a beautiful name already. Daddy and I thought about it for a long time before we named you. Normal people don't change their names all the time."

Mama glared at me. "Oh, so now I'm not normal. I'll tell you who's not normal—people who are so uptight that they can't relax and have a little fun once in a while."

"Fun? Your idea of fun is to crash through life, doing whatever makes you happy and ignoring the consequences. You don't care about anybody but yourself!" My voice had gotten louder.

Mama stood up. "Don't be so holier-than-thou with me! You know what I sacrificed for you! How dare you treat me like this!" She picked up her teacup and splashed the contents on me.

I gasped and stood up to face her. We were leaning over the table at each other, ready to scratch each others' eyes out. Something made me pause for a moment. It was a muffled sound from Amelia. She was holding her napkin up to her face, trying to hide her tears.

I sat down, feeling as deflated as though a pin had been stuck in me. What was wrong with me, acting like this in a public place? And embarrassing my daughter. I'd always sworn my children would never be ashamed of me.

"Amelia, it's all right. We're not really mad at each other. Right, Mama?" I looked up at Mama, willing her to play along. Her face was still full of righteous indignation. She saw nothing wrong with her behavior.

"Can we go home now? I'm not hungry," murmured Amelia into her napkin.

"Of course," I replied. "Let me just pay our check." I got up and went to find Celestina Luna. I'd tell her I had a sick headache. It wasn't really a lie—I could feel the throbbing start at my temples.

"You ruined our day," Mama pouted. "We were having so much fun and then you had to start a fight."

I looked at her sitting there in her yellow hat and matching gloves. Once again, it was all about her. She didn't even seem to notice Amelia's distress. I hoped Amelia remembered that.

# CHAPTER FORTY

The ride home was silent. Between Mama's sulking and Amelia's gloom, I could actually focus on my own thoughts. The outing had been a disaster, no two ways about it. My problem had been getting bullied into including Mama. If I was going to win Amelia's allegiance, I needed to do it on my terms.

I was still working on a new plan when we arrived home. Both Mama and Amelia got out of the car, slammed their doors (although I've told them dozens of times to be more careful) and stomped into the house. I sighed and gently pushed my own door shut. It was just as easy to do things the right way as the wrong way.

When I got inside, Dan was hovering in the foyer with a bewildered look on his face. "I tried to say something to both Amelia and Aunt Mae, but neither one would speak to me. They went straight to their rooms."

"It's not you, hon. They just had a little spat at the tea shop. It'll blow over. How were the girls?"

His face cleared. "They're fine. I got home about half an hour ago and they've been playing beauty parlor. I paid Suzy for a full two hours, even though she wasn't here that long. I mean, she might have given up another job to sit for us, so I wanted to be fair."

I touched his cheek gently. "You're a good man, Dan Stranahan. And I love you." A hint of sadness entered my mind when I thought of all the lies I'd told my husband, but I quickly banished such thoughts. Some things couldn't be helped.

"Anyway," he said after giving me a hug, "the main reason I wanted to talk to Aunt Mae was to let her know that Rick found out the name of Teddy's attorney, so she can get in touch with him and make sure everything goes the way Teddy would have wanted it."

My heart leapt. This might be my chance to foil Mama and her evil ways. "Umm, who is it? Anyone we know?" I asked in a nonchalant tone.

"As a matter of fact, I think you know his wife. Isn't your school psych married to an attorney? Blankenship? That's him."

"You're right. Don't worry about telling Mama now. She's too upset. I'll let her know tomorrow and then she can call him on Monday."

"Okay. Say, I like your hat, your majesty."

"Wha—oh, I forgot I had this on!" I snatched the tiara off my head. How embarrassing to think that I'd driven home wearing that trashy thing.

The rest of the evening unfolded smoothly. I made Amelia come down for dinner, even though she ate little and talked less. Mama refused to join us and stayed sequestered in her room. Dan and the little girls played a board game together—their current favorite was Hi-Ho-Cherry-O, which grated on my last nerve—while I scrubbed down the kitchen. At least once a week I like to give it a real thorough cleaning. I move the refrigerator, clean the oven, and just generally make sure everything is spotless. I was reorganizing the linen drawer when I heard someone come in. It was Mama.

"Feeling better?" I asked in a saccharine tone.

"Yes, thank you," she replied haughtily. "I thought I'd make myself a cup of soup. I believe I could manage that."

Soup! Naturally she'd want something that was messy. That

one cup of soup would involve a pan, a spoon, a cup or bowl, plus who knows how many spills and cracker crumbs—because I've never known Mama to have soup without crackers. I shut the drawer I'd been working on and pulled a pan out of the cupboard.

"Chicken noodle or tomato?"

"I *am* capable of making soup, you know."

"I'm sure. However, I've just finished cleaning the kitchen and I'd prefer that you don't undo all my work. I'll make it."

"Whatever." Mama collapsed onto a kitchen chair. "I can't stop thinking about Teddy. It's horrible that he died just as he was getting ready to propose. He would've taken care of me for the rest of my born days." She sighed.

"Huh!" I snorted. "Instead you took care of him!" I banged the top of the can opener a little harder than was necessary.

"You know, Jess," she said, her eyes narrowing, "I've had enough of your little innuendos. Somebody left that oil spilled on the deck of Teddy's boat, and I don't think it was him, and I know it wasn't me. So where were *you* that day? Did you take a day off from school? Did you spill that oil, and then hope one of us would slip and fall? Or maybe you hid out on the boat and gave him that final push. You'd do anything to hurt me, wouldn't you? Anything to destroy my dreams." She buried her face in her hands and sobbed loudly.

I felt panicky. That day was a bit of a blur to me. I'd gone to work that day—I'm sure I had. But why did I have the substitute services phone number written down on that paper by the phone? It didn't fit. It scared me to think that I might have had a lost day. That's what I used to call them when I was growing up—lost days. Every now and then, I wouldn't be able to recall exactly how I'd spent my time. I could make a good guess, based on my daily routines, but I didn't know for sure. I never told anyone about them.

Those lacunae in my days were long behind me. I knew exactly what I was doing and why every minute of the twenty-four hours allotted to me. Besides, why would I want to hurt Teddy? His death caused more complications than solutions. Now, if Mama had fallen overboard, I'd understand why anyone who knew the truth about our relationship would immediately suspect me of doing her harm. But she hadn't and I didn't—hurt anyone, that is. It was just Mama trying to confuse me.

"Here's your soup," I said brusquely, "and your crackers."

She raised her head and started to slowly lift her spoon to her mouth, one tiny sip at a time. Just as I thought, her eyes were dry. Mama, the queen of manipulation. She'd twisted me inside out when I was a child, until I didn't know what to believe. I was an adult now, and I was stronger. I could break those knots that bound us. Maybe she'd like a taste of her own medicine. Could a con be conned? I'd find out, one way or another.

"By the way, Dan said he hadn't heard from Rick yet about finding out who Teddy's attorney was. Probably because it's the weekend. Just wanted you to know that Dan hadn't blown off your problem."

She waved her hand desultorily. "No rush. Nobody else will be looking for him. Teddy didn't have any family. That's why he depended so on me."

There was no point in answering such drivel so I turned and started scrubbing the pan. Sure enough, count it—one, two, three—Mama got up and left the kitchen. Work was always a sure way to get rid of her.

# CHAPTER FORTY-ONE

*Gray clouds were rumbling across the sky and the wind was whipping the trees into a frenzy. I shivered as I stood in the road in my thin cotton dress. Mama was standing in the field beside the dirt road looking up at the sky with delight.*

*"It's storming, Jess-girl. Nobody will know. It's perfect."*

*"I'm scared, Mama. What are you talking about? Where's Sally and Grandma? They said they'd be back soon." I tried to creep closer to Mama but she saw me.*

*"Don't cling, girl!" Mama's voice rang with anger. "I can't stand clinging!" She strode away across the field.*

*"Mama, I'm sorry. I'll be good. Don't leave me!" To my shame, I started to cry.*

*Suddenly I was sitting in a church, listening to a pale man in a black suit read from the Bible. "Earth to earth, ashes to ashes, dust to dust." I put my hands over my ears so I wouldn't have to hear the horrible words and squeezed my eyes shut so I could pretend to be somewhere else.*

*Mama elbowed me sharply. "Sit up straight and look intelligent. You're embarrassing me. He wasn't your real daddy anyway."*

*Her words had their desired effect. I sat up straight and stared at her. "But you said Matt was better'n my real daddy. You said—"*

*"I said hush up, and I mean business." She was talking in a low furious whisper. "You can't depend on no man, not any of 'em. Now we gotta get through this like ladies, and then we'll have some fun. Just sit there and look sad."*

*My head was spinning like a tilt-a-whirl. I didn't have to pretend to be sad, I was sad. How come Mama wasn't? She acted sad when Baby Nate died. Was she just faking then, too? I knew she didn't care anything about my real daddy, but I could barely remember him. I looked out the church window. The sky was dark, thunder clouds looming overhead. A flash of lightning split the heavens in two like a jagged knife cut. I leaned back against the hard wooden pew. It was good to feel something real.*

I sat up in bed in a cold sweat. It took me a minute to orient myself. Yes, this was my own bed with the soft cotton sheets. Dan was beside me, snoring gently. I touched my face and hair. Yes, I was the grownup Jess, not the pitiful Jess-girl who was so dependent on the fickle love of Mama.

I slipped out of bed and padded into the bathroom. As I poured myself a glass of water, I debated whether or not to take one of Dan's sleeping pills. On the one hand, it would assure me of getting back to sleep. On the other hand, the drug information said it might cause vivid dreams. I shook my head and drank the plain water. No thanks, I could do vivid dreams all on my own.

The question was what to do now that I was wide awake. The bedside clock read three thirty-seven. Too early to get up, but too late to try for a deep sleep. I put on my robe and slippers and tiptoed down the stairs. The novel I'd been trying to finish for my book club was in the living room. Maybe it would put me to sleep—it certainly hadn't kept my attention so far.

Entering the living room, I saw my purse on the hall table. My key ring was hanging out. Of course! I'd take a drive. It might relax me, and it would at the very least kill some time until I could officially start the day. Should I get dressed? No, I wouldn't be stopping anywhere. Besides, Dan said my robe would put a nun to shame. It was definitely not revealing.

I slipped out the front door and took a minute to enjoy the silence of the night. Our little suburban neighborhood had been a haven for me, providing the type of life I'd always dreamed of as a young, lonely girl. I loved hearing the lawn mowers on Saturday, seeing children ride their bikes, waving hello to neighbors as I picked up the mail. Of course, I wasn't really close with any of them. It was dangerous to become too intimate with people. Just as I had secrets to hide, perhaps they did, also. It was exhausting enough to maintain my relationship with Dan, let alone try to juggle friendships.

I shook my head to clear the cobwebs and headed for my car. Since all the bedrooms but Mama's were upstairs, and hers was in the back of the house, no one should hear me start the engine. I eased the car door open and slid into the seat. Just to be on the safe side, I didn't turn the headlights on until I was on the street.

There were no other cars on the road in our neighborhood, and very few when I turned onto the main thoroughfare. It was soothing to drive with no destination in mind and hardly any traffic to worry about. I felt safe and snug in my metal shell, as though nothing and no one could harm me. What would it be like just to keep driving, maybe all the way to the coast? I started dreamily humming my favorite beach song, "Good Vibrations."

I turned down a dark side street as though on autopilot. There was a parking lot straight ahead, and I guided the car into it. I had my pick of parking places. The only other vehicle was a semi-trailer truck that looked long abandoned. I gazed around in bewilderment. Where was I? Why was I here? There was a sign off to the left that read "Mulhaven Yacht Club." I recalled Mama saying this was where Teddy had kept his boat, but I'd never been here.

With a troubled mind, I parked and got out of the car. I wasn't too upset to remember to click the lock—you could never be too careful. I pulled my robe tight against the cold wind coming off the water and walked toward the dark building that sat on the edge of the marina. It was the yacht club, of course, and it seemed vaguely familiar. Had I been here before? No, I wouldn't have forgotten something like that. I found a bench overlooking the basin and sat down.

The rippling water didn't calm, but instead seemed to mirror my thoughts. They were coming and going without my volition. I shut my eyes and tried to visualize when I might have been here before. Dreamlike fragments came and went—Mama and Teddy, dressed to the nines; the rocking of a boat under my feet; the shock of icy cold water as I swam desperately toward shore.

I shook my head in frustration. Had I been here when Mama pushed Teddy overboard? I had no doubt that she had done so, but I was concluding that based on my knowledge of her and her ways. There was no way I had witnessed the murder. I couldn't allow myself to confront the possibility that my lacunae—my blank spots—had returned. No, it wasn't a memory, more likely a scrap of a dream.

The sky was beginning to lighten. I checked my watch and saw it was just past four thirty. There was no time to sit here and indulge myself with pointless imaginings. I needed to get back to my family. I had responsibilities. I hurried to my car and started toward home.

# CHAPTER FORTY-TWO

I made it home just before the arrival of the Sunday paper. I hurried upstairs and jumped in the shower. Sure enough, Dan was dead to the world until he heard the water running. As I stepped out and toweled myself off, I could hear him grunting his way through his crunches. I smiled to myself. Poor dear, he was trying so hard. My resolve strengthened. I wouldn't let anyone jeopardize his blissful ignorance.

I stepped into the bedroom. "I bought some fresh blueberries yesterday. How about pancakes for breakfast?"

He stood up and hugged me. "What did I do to deserve a wife like you?" I smiled and patted his cheek, thinking *I hope you never find out.*

I decided to let the girls sleep in since it was Sunday. We never went to church except for Christmas and Easter. Even then, I made sure we visited different congregations. I had no desire to join the true believers. There was one foster home where the dad was a preacher, and I learned enough about hypocrisy and wolves in sheep's clothing to turn me off organized religion for a lifetime. My children were taught everything they needed to know about morals and ethical behavior by me.

I was folding the blueberries into the batter when Amelia came in. She sat at the kitchen table and watched me work. Finally I couldn't stand the silence any longer.

"You're up early," I said in a neutral tone. "Did you sleep well?"

"I guess." She shrugged her shoulders. "Mama, why don't you and Grandma like each other? Is it because of how your dad raised you—to hate her, I mean?"

Brother! Now I was going to have to keep Mama's lies straight, as well as my own misdirections. There *was* a difference between the two. She lied when the truth would do better, and I simply omitted facts that would cause trouble. I sighed and tried to think how to answer Amelia's question.

"Well, honey, it's sort of hard to explain. Growing up without a mom, I learned to depend on myself. Now I have to get used to having a mother again. It takes some adjustment. But you shouldn't worry. Your grandma and I will work things out." I bent down and cupped her chin so that she had to look up at me. "And I'm sorry for the way we acted at the tea room. That was very immature of—us." I stopped myself from blaming Mama, even though she'd started the whole scene. Pointing the finger at Mama would only push Amelia away.

As long as we were having a heart-to-heart, I decided to probe a little bit. I sat down at the table beside her.

"Amelia, you know you can tell me anything, right?"

She gave me a doubtful look but nodded her head.

"And you know that you can trust me to guide you in the right direction whenever you get confused or upset. I'm your mother, and no one will ever love you like I do. Sometimes I have to discipline you, but it's only because I love you. You know that, right?"

"Sure, Mama. I know you only have my best interests at heart." She said it mechanically, by rote. I guess I'd used that phrase once too often.

I leaned toward her and took her hands in mine. "Amelia, honey, what happened to Grandma's bird? I'm sure it was an accident, but what happened? You can tell me. It'll be our secret."

She jumped up so fast she knocked the chair over. "I didn't do it! It wasn't me! I thought it was you! You're the one who hated Sunshine. Or maybe it was Amanda or Abigail—they're so dumb, they probably squeezed it to death. You always blame me! I hate you!"

I sat in stunned silence as she raced out of the room and upstairs. At my lowest, I'd never told Mama that I hated her, and I certainly had more cause than Amelia did. With those words, she'd thrown all my sacrifices in my face. She didn't care about how hard I worked to give her a perfect childhood. It was time to admit the truth—Amelia was more like Mama than she ever would be like me. As proof, she'd lied to my face when I was being understanding and compassionate. Just like Mama, she'd tried to blame others, even her innocent little sisters, rather than accept the consequences of her actions.

Dan came in while I was still brooding. He had a concerned look on his face.

"What's up with Amelia? She ran past me like a whirlwind. What happened?"

I stood up and pasted on a smile. "Better get used to it, honey. I think her hormones are starting to emerge."

"But she's only ten," he said in bewilderment.

"Girls grow up fast these days, and besides, she's eleven. Don't fret. We'll get through it."

He nodded, eager to accept my reassurance. "Pancakes almost ready?" he said hopefully.

"Give me ten minutes. Now shoo!" I turned to the stove and began to heat up the griddle.

I spent the day finding tasks to do outside so that I could avoid Mama and Amelia. They were both determined to make everybody else as miserable as they were. I finally sent Amanda and Abigail out to weed the back garden just get them out of the line of fire. Of course, I knew that the little girls could barely distinguish a weed from a vegetable, but better that than having them come crying to me every two minutes because Amelia had insulted them.

As usual on a Sunday, Dan was sprawled on the couch watching sports. I didn't exactly resent him for doing so; it was more that I didn't understand it. I could no more sit back and let someone else work around me than fly to the moon. It wasn't that he took me for granted—he always remembered to thank me when I'd bring him a drink and snacks—he was simply oblivious. And mind you, it didn't even matter what kind of sporting event was on. He preferred basketball or football, but Yugoslavian underwater volleyball would do just as well.

Much as I loved him, it was obvious that I carried the heavier load in the marriage. I kept our lives organized, our house clean, our children healthy. I scheduled our doctor appointments and even sent birthday and Mother's Day cards to his mother, handing them to him for a signature right before mailing. I was the one who stayed home to wait for repairmen and hovered around to make sure they did the job right. Early in our marriage, I'd worked in Dan's office as a receptionist, juggling that with finishing my teaching courses. When I stopped to think about it, it was no wonder that I'd taken that little break a few weeks ago to my favorite hotel. Everyone needs some pampering now and then.

Sighing, I picked up my pruning shears and headed out to the front yard. My poor roses had been neglected long enough. I'd just gotten started when Dan called from inside the house.

"Honey! Honey, can you come here for a minute?"

"What now," I mumbled to myself. I dusted off my knees and went in the front door. I was met with bedlam. Mama was on the living room couch weeping, Amelia was running up the stairs screaming, the two little girls were standing in the mud they'd tracked in, and Dan was all but wringing his hands.

"Jess, everybody's gone crazy! I don't know what's going on."

I stood in the entry and raised the pruning shears up like a sword. "Stop it right this minute!" I bellowed. It worked. My family had never heard me raise my voice before. It felt great. Everyone froze and looked at me, then at the pruning shears, then back at me. I lowered the shears.

"Amelia, go to your room and stay there until I come up to talk to you. Mama, same thing. We'll talk when you've calmed down. Girls, get the broom and sweep up that dirt. Dan, turn off the damn TV and back me up. I can't do everything by myself."

He rushed into the family room and turned off the game that had been blaring in the background.

"What can I do to help?" he asked.

I hugged him. "Just be here and let me know I'm loved."

He hugged me back. "No problem there. You know I love you, Jess. I don't know how you do everything you do. The way you calmed everybody down—it's like you're a miracle worker."

I smiled and leaned into him. "I know why Amelia's upset, but what got Mama going?"

"I'm not really sure. I said something to her about Rick finding out the name of Teddy's attorney, and she went ballistic, started crying about lies and deceit. That got Amelia going, and before you know it—kapow—a perfect storm of feminine rage." He raised both hands in front of him in an "I give up" gesture.

I winced. So Mama found out I'd lied to her about the lawyer. That meant she'd be on the phone early Monday morning, before I'd have a chance to contact him first. My plan had been to get some information from him before Mama weaseled her way in. Oh, well, it couldn't be helped. I squared my shoulders.

The only question now was which Herculean task I should tackle first—Scylla or Charybdis.

# CHAPTER FORTY-THREE

I decided to confront Mama first. In some ways, it was easier to deal with her than with Amelia. Mama's tricks were so obvious to me that it was almost laughable. Amelia, on the other hand, was unpredictable. Perhaps it was because I kept stubbornly expecting her to respond to her upbringing instead of going down the same road as her grandmother. Giving up my idealized view of Amelia was almost like death. I'd need to strengthen myself before I talked with her.

I knocked on Mama's door but opened it before she had a chance to respond. She was sitting on her bed with her strongbox open beside her, its contents strewn on the comforter. She tried to snatch the papers up but I was too fast for her.

"Hold it right there. You've been keeping enough secrets, like that fake ID. I deserve to know what's going on with you." I grabbed the half-empty box and held it in front of me like a shield.

"I don't owe you anything. I already gave you my freedom."

"Please. You didn't give up anything for me. I admit I don't remember everything about Nathan's death, but if I had anything to do with it, it was an accident. When I fed him that whiskey, I was only doing what I'd seen you do a hundred times. You've used that lie to bind me tighter to you, but it can't hold me anymore."

She stood up, enraged. "Lie? You dare to talk to me about a lie? You lie to me all the time. Why didn't you tell me about

Teddy's attorney? What could you possibly have to gain by keeping that information from me?"

I wasn't sure how to respond. The truth was, I wasn't sure why it had seemed important to get the jump on Mama with the attorney. I hadn't thought what I'd say to him, or what privileged communication I hoped he'd share with me. Thinking about it now, the whole plan seemed ridiculous. But there was no way I'd admit that to Mama.

"I don't know what you're talking about. I didn't say anything to you about any lawyer. Go ahead and call him tomorrow. It's nothing to do with me." I stood calmly, making my bluff more plausible.

Mama's mouth gaped open like a goldfish. She didn't have anything to say for a change. I rushed in before she could regain control.

"You'll make a fool of yourself with that attorney. What are you going to say, 'I was Teddy's girlfriend so I'm entitled to his estate'? That sounds plausible."

"That's all you know!" exclaimed Mama, brandishing a paper in front of her. "This happens to be a holographic will where Teddy says I am his sole heir. We both made them as a symbol of our commitment to each other."

Now I was the one with my mouth open. "How did you talk him into that?" I finally managed. "You don't have anything to leave anyone."

"Now how would you know that, unless you've been snooping in my private property?" She gathered up the strewn papers from the bed. "Give me my strongbox. I'll feel better when I have things under lock and key."

I handed over the box and watched as she began to stuff papers into it. I couldn't help myself; I had to know, even if it meant admitting that I had snooped.

"Mama," I said hesitantly, "there are letters addressed to me in there, aren't there."

She looked up at me in shock. "So you have been sneaking around behind my back! What if there are? You don't care about how I agonized over you while I was locked up."

I sat down on the bed, and she sat beside me. "Did you really care, Mama? Were you worried about me?" My voice didn't sound like itself. It was almost as if I'd been transformed into that lonely little girl of my past.

"Of course I worried about you. You're a part of me, you're my daughter. *Mine,*" she emphasized. "The two of us are bound together for life. There's no tie closer than mother and daughter."

I drew back in revulsion. The last thing I wanted to hear was that I was like Mama in any way. I'd struggled to form my own identity, and I wasn't going to lose it now.

I stood up and spoke, my voice cold. "You're wrong, Mama. It's not ties you're talking about—it's chains. I was chained to you for years, but no more. I'm my own person now. I'm nothing like you. I don't push people around to get what I want or think only of myself and my needs. No, I'm nothing like you."

Mama sat on the bed, looking at me with a knowing smile. "Whatever you say, dear heart. Whatever you say."

I turned and fled the room. My heart was pounding, and I knew I had to calm down before I saw Amelia. I rushed into the kitchen and gulped down a glass of ice water. Looking around the perfectly appointed room, I felt myself calming. There was my beautiful stainless steel refrigerator, my double oven, my granite countertops. Everything was sparkling clean. This was my life, not Mama's messy slop of existence. I rinsed out the glass and put it in the dishwasher. I was ready now.

As I reached the top of the stairs, I saw to my surprise that Amelia's door was open. I'd expected her to be hiding inside her room, trying to block out the family. Instead, she sat primly on her bed, hands folded, ankles crossed.

"Hello, Mama," she said in a clear, confident voice, looking me straight in the eyes.

I managed not to show my consternation at her aplomb. "I'm glad to see you've calmed down, Amelia. Are you ready to talk about your inappropriate behavior?"

"Mama, you were right. I did hurt Sunshine. I didn't mean to kill him, it just happened. And then I was scared to tell."

She didn't look scared. She looked like—well, to say she looked like the cat that ate the canary would be morbid, but something along those lines.

I took a step back. Something about the way she was staring at me discomfited me. "I'm glad you've decided to take responsibility for your actions. It's probably the guilt over Sunshine's death that has made you so upset lately."

"Guilt?" She wrinkled her brow. "No, I don't think so. Why should I feel guilty? It wasn't really my fault. I was just trying to make him be quiet—for you, Mama. I knew his chirping bothered you."

"Well, whatever the reason, now you have to tell Grandma what happened. Then it will all be behind you."

Amelia stood up and faced me. "Oh, no, Mama. I'm not going to tell her. I don't want Grandma to be mad at me. She thinks you did it anyway. Even if you told her it was me, I bet she wouldn't believe you. I just wanted you to know the real truth, Mama. That's all. You said we shouldn't have secrets."

"I'll—I'll consider what you've said," I managed to stutter out. "I'll decide what the best course of action will be." I turned and walked steadily out of her room. I couldn't let her see how she'd rattled me. Now there was no denying it. Amelia and Mama were cut from the same cloth, and I was the only one who could do something about it.

# CHAPTER FORTY-FOUR

The next day was a typical Monday. I hurried the girls through dressing and breakfast and got us out the door early. I felt oppressed by the house. Mama's presence was the cause, I knew. She had infected my sanctuary against the world, and she had succeeded in infecting my daughter as well.

Once at school, I put all thoughts of home and family inside a mental box and went into full teacher mode. I'd learned long ago to compartmentalize my emotions in this way. It was the only way I was able to survive the foster home years.

My students were busy with a worksheet and the room was gratifyingly quiet when Amy Blankenship, the school psychologist, walked in. She came close and spoke in a low voice.

"I'd like to talk some things over with you. When do the kids go to their special?"

I frowned. "I turned that paperwork in on Jimmy. Didn't you get it?"

"Paperwork—oh, right. No, it's not about him. It's actually about Amelia." Her broad earnest face showed concern—and was that pity? It had better not be.

"They go to P.E. at ten forty-five. I'll have twenty-five minutes."

"Thanks ever so. I'm sure we'll get everything worked out." She reached out to squeeze my hand but dropped hers awkwardly when I kept mine at my sides. She waved briefly as she left the classroom.

I was in agony until the class went to P.E. My reliable trick of locking unpleasantness away failed me. What had Amelia done? What signs was she exhibiting? She'd been so strange lately that I couldn't guess what deviousness she'd been up to.

I was just unlocking my door after taking the students to P.E. when Amy walked up. I ushered her in silently and nodded for her to take a seat. She had to squeeze herself into a student desk since there were no other chairs. I took my customary place behind my teacher desk.

"Well?" I finally said when she seemed reluctant to begin. I must admit I enjoyed watching her squirm uncomfortably in the miniscule seat.

"Jess, first let me say that I think you're an outstanding teacher and a caring mother. I've seen how conscientious you are with your daughters. But sometimes children can exhibit behaviors that may be due to all sorts of reasons—biochemical, allergies, and things that we just can't explain." She paused to take a breath.

I quickly jumped in before she could take up more time with her delaying tactics. "Please get to the point, Amy. What exactly is wrong? What has Amelia done?"

"It's a little hard to explain. Amelia's behavior has undergone some subtle shifts since the beginning of the year. She's still an excellent student, especially in language arts, but her attitude toward both her teacher and fellow students has changed. She's always been such a shy little thing, but now she's quite asser-tive. In fact, her teacher has noticed that she has become a leader with the other girls—almost a ringleader, you might say." Amy laughed nervously.

"A ringleader? That's a word with a very negative connota-tion, Ms. Blankenship." I wasn't going to act like this was just a friendly chat between colleagues.

Amy sat up as straight as she could in her confined seat.

"Jess, she exerts quite a hold over the others. They've all decided to exclude one little girl, and Amelia is the one who makes up hurtful names and rhymes about her. Ms. Barnes spoke to her, of course—in fact, to all of them—about being unkind. She said that some of the girls seemed remorseful, but Amelia just stared at her. And the staring has continued. In class, she'll look out on the class and Amelia and her followers will just be staring at her, almost without blinking. She said it's very unnerving."

I got up from my desk and began pacing. "This is disgraceful! Why didn't Ms. Barnes come to me directly? There was no reason to speak with the school psychologist over some silly childish pranks."

Amy struggled to her feet also. "She didn't come to me. I was doing a classroom observation and saw the behavior for myself. I questioned her about it later. I could see she was upset. When I asked her if she had spoken to you, she said that Amelia had said something about someone named Aunt Mae causing you extra stress. She didn't want to add to your burden."

I was furious, but I wasn't sure who was the cause. Amelia, for her unacceptable behavior? Kathy Barnes, for being too weak to control her students? Amy Blankenship, for her gall in discussing this with me? Or Mama, for upsetting my carefully stacked family applecart?

Taking a deep breath, I realized that my anger knew no bounds. I had plenty to go around for all concerned.

"Thank you for bringing this to my attention. I'll handle things at home with Amelia. I have to go retrieve my students now. I don't think we'll need to discuss this again." I walked briskly toward the door.

"Jess, if there's anything I can do, you know I'm available. Maybe I could talk with Amelia. You know, sometimes children feel more open with a non-family member."

I turned and gave her a steely gaze. "Do not talk to my

daughter without my permission. If you try, I'll see that you lose your license." I waited until she left the room before I followed suit.

I managed to get through the rest of the day. I spoke in monosyllables to the girls when I bundled them into the car at the close of school. As I drove, I surreptitiously eyed all three in the rearview mirror. Amelia was sitting between her two sisters, telling them something in a low voice. They both nodded, wide-eyed. I couldn't have her influencing my sweet babies, I just couldn't. As we pulled up to the house, I spoke.

"Amelia, I need to speak with you for a minute. Abigail and Amanda, go in and put your things away." The two little ones raced out of the car. Amelia slumped back against the backseat with a bored expression on her face.

I turned and looked at her. "Amelia, I know about the bullying you've been doing at school. It needs to stop right now. And I don't want to hear about any disrespect of your teacher. Are we clear?"

She sat up, ready to defend herself. "I haven't done anything wrong! That dumb old Ms. Barnes has been lying to you!"

"I haven't spoken with your teacher about this at all."

Amelia's face darkened. "Then it was that psycho lady—Mrs. Blankenship. She was nosing around in our class. I bet it was her, wasn't it?" Something in my face must have given me away, because she nodded in satisfaction.

"I knew it! She always acts like she likes kids, but she really doesn't. She lies, Mama! She just wants to get me in trouble!"

"Amelia, that's enough," I said sharply. "We've discussed this, and it's over. I don't expect to get any more bad reports about you from now on. Go inside. I'll be there in a minute."

She scrambled out of the car, slamming the door as I had expected she would. I watched her go inside the house and slam that door, too. I sighed to myself. I was going to have to watch Amelia very carefully. I'd been lulled into thinking that she was like me, when all along a ticking time bomb was inside her. I couldn't let that time bomb go off. I would need to be more vigilant than ever.

# Chapter Forty-Five

Dinner that night was our new usual. That is, I served a nutritious and well-cooked meal while Mama monopolized the conversation. The girls occasionally got a word in edgewise but she acknowledged them only briefly. Tonight she was flying high after her conversation with Teddy's attorney, Roger Blankenship. Amelia's eyes widened when she heard his last name but she quickly put her head down. Dan was humoring Mama in her carrying-on.

"So he was expecting to hear from you?" he asked, scooping up a forkful of ginger chicken stir-fry, one of my specialties. The secret is fresh ginger.

"My dear, he was positively thrilled when I called!" Mama dimpled. "He said he had some instructions from Teddy concerning me and that he'd go over everything in detail tomorrow when we meet at his office. Just think, I might be moving into my own little place soon! I know Teddy wanted me to be provided for."

Dan nodded, but before he could speak I broke in. "I think you're jumping the gun. Mr. Blankenship said he had instructions about you, not an inheritance. That could mean just about anything."

"Aunt Mae, we don't want you to move!" wailed Amanda. "You don't need your own little place. Our house is big enough for all of us."

Mama and I locked eyes. "Darlin', you're a little young to

understand, but sometimes a house can't be big enough for two women. Anyway, I'd still come to visit. You three girls are as dear to me as if you were my own grandchildren." She sat back with a satisfied smirk.

I stood up abruptly and started clearing the table. "We have homemade almond cookies for dessert. Amelia, would you bring them out, please? They're on the platter by the stove."

Amelia slowly got up from her chair and inched her way into the kitchen. I knew she was trying to bait me so I held my tongue and busied myself with the dishes. Every battle won was a step closer to winning the war.

With dinner over and homework done, the girls were watching TV with Mama. They were allowed one show a night on school nights and had to take turns choosing it. Tonight was Abigail's turn and she had picked some silly dancing show. I stayed in the kitchen, cleaning the refrigerator. I had my back to the door and so didn't hear Dan sneaking up on me.

"Gotcha!" he laughed, wrapping me in a bear hug.

"Dan, you almost gave me a heart attack!" I said, dropping my sponge and a bottle of cleanser. "I'm busy here, if you didn't notice."

He gave me a sheepish grin. "I know, but I'm bored. I can't stand that *Dancing with the Has-Beens* show."

I smiled and patted his cheek. "Sit down and I'll get you some ice cream."

He readily complied and gave an appreciative sigh when I placed the bowl of ice cream in front of him. I watched him eat and suddenly felt a wave of melancholy.

"Dan, what would you do if I wasn't here?"

He looked up in alarm. "What do you mean? You're not going away again, are you? Because I can tell you, Jess, that was awful. I was so worried, not knowing where you were or if you were okay."

"No, I mean, what if I died before you? Unexpectedly? What would you do?"

"Jess, honey, what brought this on? Don't be so morbid. You're not going to die any time soon. We'll grow old together, with matching rocking chairs." He dropped his spoon and grabbed my hands.

I sat down beside him. "It's not morbid. It's something we should discuss. How would you cope with the girls, the house, everything?" I wrenched my hands free and waved them in the air, taking in all the responsibilities that would be his.

"Well, I'd need help, I know," he gulped. "But there's Aunt Mae, and my mom. They'd be there, I know. And I'd probably have to hire a housekeeper. You know, we could do that now, except you always say you don't need one."

"I don't." I sat quietly for a moment. Mama and his mother— that would be quite a pair. My mother-in-law was as prim and proper as you could get. That's why she had always approved of me. I could handle her helping to raise the girls, but Mama? No way.

"Jess, what about you? What would you do if I were gone?"

I forced a smile. "I'd just keep on keeping on. I'd make sure your memory was alive for the girls. Would you do the same for me?"

"Of course I would. It wouldn't be hard. Your daughters would never forget you. Everybody says you're the perfect mother." His face was anxious. He wasn't sure why I had brought this subject up, but he was doing his best to reassure me.

"I'm sorry, honey. I don't know what came over me. You're right. We'll grow old together and have a peaceful old age." I kissed his cheek. "Now finish your ice cream and let me get back to work."

He was so eager to please that he even rinsed out his bowl in the sink when he was done. As he left the kitchen to go and get the girls started on bedtime, I felt a pain in my heart. An oppressive feeling of darkness came over me. I scrubbed the inside of the refrigerator even more vigorously, but I couldn't wash away my fear.

# CHAPTER FORTY-SIX

"Oh, I'm just so excited to see Mr. Blankenship that I can't see straight," squealed Mama at breakfast. "My appointment is at nine thirty. That will barely give me time to make myself presentable."

"How are you getting there? Do you need me to drive you?" I asked as I cut Amanda's pancakes for her.

"No, no, I'm calling a cab. You've given up enough time for me. I'm perfectly capable of doing this on my own." She got up and pushed her chair in. "I'd better get a move on if I want to be ready." She left the room without bothering to clear her dirty dishes. I sighed. Why should I have expected anything else?

Dan was already gone as the girls and I were rushing around to get ready to leave. I shooed the girls out the door and told them to get in the car. With some hesitation I knocked on Mama's door.

"Mama?"

The door swung open. "What is it, Jess? I'm in a hurry, and my hair won't do what it's supposed to."

I looked at her, all dolled up in a pale gray suit. She didn't have her shoes on yet, but I could see a pair of high heels sitting on the floor by the bed. She was pulling out all the stops to impress this attorney. I wondered what was in store for her.

"I just wanted to say good luck."

She laughed. "There's no luck about it, Jess. What Mama wants, Mama gets. You know that." She shut the door.

I was eating my lunch in my classroom, glad of a brief respite in a busy day. I usually preferred this to going into the gossipy environs of the staff lunchroom. So many of the teachers, especially the younger ones, seemed to have nothing better to do than to sit around and make silly jokes at others' expense. I knew that they had different nicknames for me, ones that I didn't repeat even in my mind, but they didn't bother me. I could take pride in a well-run classroom, respectful students, and top test scores. If that meant I was known as "The Anal Queen," so be it.

I was just gathering my lunch things when I heard a siren. That was unusual on the quiet street where our school was located. Shrugging my shoulders, I threw my apple core into the trash and went to wash my hands. It was probably nothing. But the siren grew louder until it whined to a stop. It sounded like it was right at our school. Checking my watch, I saw that I still had ten minutes before the children were due back from recess. I decided to walk up to the front office and see what was going on.

I was just leaving my room when a call came on the intercom: "Ms. Stranahan, please come to the nurse's office." What had happened? Was Amelia hurt? I rushed to the nurse's office, pushing the door open so violently that it hit the wall behind it. Amelia was sitting on a cot, her eyes red-rimmed.

"Amelia! Are you all right? What happened?" I wrapped my arms around her.

She wriggled away. "I'm okay, Mama. It's not me. It's that psycho lady, Ms. Blankenship. She got real sick. I think she might die."

For the first time I noticed that Amelia and I were alone in the little room. Where were the paramedics? Even the nurse was gone. I stood back and looked straight in Amelia's eyes. She shifted them to avoid my gaze.

"What exactly happened, Amelia? And I want the truth, young lady."

Before she could respond, the nurse came in. "Oh, Jess, I'm glad you're here. Poor little Amelia is in shock, I think. She was right there when Amy Blankenship got violently ill. I don't think it was a seizure exactly, but it seemed like one. She blacked out and everything. Amelia's the one who ran for help. I think you'd better take her home for some TLC. We'll cover your class for you."

"Is Amy going to be all right? Does she have some sort of medical condition?" I kept my voice calm and steady.

"She regained consciousness by the time the paramedics got here, but of course we won't know for sure how she is until she's thoroughly checked out at the hospital. It is the strangest thing. I was talking to her just this morning, and she was fine. I'm wondering if it was some kind of botulism or food poisoning or something, because her lunch was scattered all over the floor. Thank goodness our little rescuer was nearby. I hate to think what would have happened if Amy had been alone when she lost consciousness." She smiled fondly at Amelia.

"Doris, I think you're right. I'd better take Amelia home. My plans for the afternoon are on the whiteboard. The students know exactly what they are supposed to be doing. If someone can just sit in the classroom, they won't have to do a thing."

The nurse patted my shoulder. "Don't you worry, Jess. Just take this little sweetheart home and let her relax. Maybe a bowl of ice cream might help." She winked.

"Yes, of course, that's a great idea. Let's go, Amelia." I held out my hand to her.

Reluctantly Amelia got up from the cot. She didn't take my

hand, but I don't think Doris noticed. I hustled her out of the nurse's office, and once I had signed out, we were on our way.

I didn't say anything on the drive home, and neither did Amelia. My thoughts were racing. Why had Amelia been near Amy's office? She made no secret of her dislike for the woman she called the "psycho lady." Was it possible that she had somehow caused Amy's collapse? No, that was ridiculous. She was just a child. I suddenly flashed on Sunshine's lifeless body and a chill went down my back.

When we got home I still didn't say anything. I just pointed up the stairs to her room. She slowly made her way up the stairs. I stood in the entry for a while, trying to gather my thoughts and plan my next move.

"Darlin' girl, why are you home so early? Is Amelia sick?" Mama came waltzing up to me. She'd changed out of her suit and now was sporting a fluorescent-green halter top with matching shorts. Her toes had cotton balls stuck in between them. She saw me looking at them and giggled.

"I was just giving myself a pedicure. Once things get straightened out with Teddy's will, I'll be able to afford to have mani-pedis in a salon every week."

I made a fast decision. "Mama, here's my car keys and my credit card. Why don't you go and get a mani-pedi right now."

It didn't take her long to grab the keys and the card out of my outstretched hand. "You are the best daughter ever! I promise I'll be careful with the car. There's a cute little nail salon in the shopping center. I won't be gone long. Let me just get these cotton balls out of the way and I'll be on my way. Ta-ta!"

Once she was safely out the door, I made my way up the stairs to Amelia's room. Something would come to me. I'd play it by ear.

I opened her door. "Amelia, I want you to tell me exactly

what happened today at school. Don't leave out anything."

She was sitting on the bed with her legs tucked underneath her. "Well, let's see. First I played a game of tetherball until the bell rang to come in, then I went to my desk and sat down. Ms. Barnes said get out your math books, so I—"

I resisted the urge to strike her. "Don't be a smart aleck! You know what I mean. What were you doing hanging around Mrs. Blankenship's office? I thought you hated her."

"Oh, that. Well, I just was walking down the hall because I took the attendance up to the office for Ms. Barnes—she always forgets about it—and when I went past that lady's office I saw her fall down. I asked her if she was okay but she didn't say anything so I thought I better get the nurse." She looked up at me with wide innocent eyes. What was it that was different about her? Of course: her hair. It wasn't covering her face like a curtain, the way I'd grown accustomed to seeing her. She had it pushed back with a hair band, so that she was open to the world. This must mean something, but I wasn't sure if it was a good sign or a bad omen.

"Are you sure that's what happened? Is there anything else I need to know?"

"No, Mama. I told you everything you need to know. Can I have some ice cream now? The nurse said it would be good for me."

I put my hand to my head and then turned to leave the room. "Come on," I said over my shoulder. "I'm not bringing it to you."

She leaped off the bed and followed me. "I scream, you scream, we all scream for ice cream," she sang lustily. If only Nurse Doris could see poor, traumatized Amelia now, I mused. She'd be shocked at her miraculous recovery.

# CHAPTER FORTY-SEVEN

Dinner that night was interesting. I expected Mama to come home from her mani-pedi treat full of gossip and giggles, but she was in a bad mood. She kept waiting for the phone to ring, and when dinnertime came around and she still hadn't heard from Mr. Blankenship, she was in a huff. Amelia, on the other hand, was chatty and high-spirited. She even laughed at Abigail's attempt at a knock-knock joke. It made me uneasy to see her that way. I was used to the old, sulky Amelia. I wasn't quite sure what to make of her new personality.

After dessert Mama retired to her room. I suppose I should have told her about Amy Blankenship's illness, so she'd understand why the lawyer hadn't called her back, but I didn't feel up to discussing the matter. I figured she'd find out soon enough. I waited to see if Amelia would say anything about it, but she was excited about being in charge of the TV viewing for the night. It was a relief not to have to talk it over with Dan. I still had unanswered questions myself.

Later that night as I was tucking Amelia in bed, she suddenly sat up. "Mama, are you going to the store tomorrow?"

"I might. Why?"

"Because I need some supplies. I'm almost out of pencil lead, and I need a highlighter—oh, yeah, and some more tissues and hand sanitizer."

"Hand sanitizer? Last year that little bottle lasted you the whole school year."

"I know, because you're only supposed to use a few drops. But I lost mine. I can't find it anywhere. It probably fell out of my backpack, or maybe someone stole it."

I laughed. "I doubt that anyone would steal your hand sanitizer. Remind me to stop by the drugstore on our way home tomorrow."

"Okay, Mama. G'night."

"Lights out in ten minutes."

As I left her room, something kept plaguing my thoughts. It was something to do with hand sanitizer. What was it? It was just on the tip of my memory. Perhaps it was some ad or something. It couldn't be that important.

*I was jumping rope, singing. "Did you ever see a hearse go by? Then you will be the next to die. The worms go in, the worms go out—" I stopped jumping and sat down on the rope. "I don't like that rhyme. It's scary."*

*Mama and Amelia had been twirling the rope and they both started laughing. "Cry baby!" taunted Mama.*

*"Yeah, cry baby," echoed Amelia.*

*I stood up and stomped my foot. "I'm not a cry baby! I just like nice things, happy things. You two are gross!"*

*They both came closer to me, clutching the rope in their hands. "They wrap you up in a bloody sheet, and throw you down about fifty feet, then the worms crawl in, the worms crawl out, the worms are crawling all about." They started winding the jump rope around me, confining my arms to my side.*

*"Stop it!" I cried. "You're hurting me!"*

*"Oh, no, dear, these are the ties that bind. The three of us are bound together forever—grandmother, mother, daughter. You'll never break free." Mama's voice was kind and gentle.*

*"No, that's not true! I can get away! I'm not like you! I'm not!"*

I sat up in bed. Thank God I'd snapped out of it. What a strange, horrid nightmare! I lay down again, determined to get back to a dreamless sleep on my own. I started counting backward from one hundred.

". . . eighty-nine, eighty-eight—oh, my God!" My eyes popped open. It suddenly came to me. I remembered why hand sanitizer had been lurking in my memory.

We had a special staff meeting at school a few months back. A local drug education agency had come in to inform us about some of the common household substances that were being abused by teenagers in the community—cleaning supplies, mouthwash, correction fluid—and hand sanitizer. I hadn't paid a lot of attention since my students were too young for such nonsense, but I remembered telling Dan about it at dinner that same night.

"Can you imagine having to lock up your air fresheners or office supplies because you can't trust your own children? And some kids even try to get intoxicated from hand sanitizer. They said there'd been at least two deaths from that. I'm so glad that we know how to parent properly. Our daughters will never need to escape into drugs, because they're being raised correctly."

"Hand sanitizer?" Dan had asked, wrinkling his nose. "What's the kick in that?"

"It has alcohol in it. These poor misguided teenagers think they'll get high, but they end up extremely sick or even worse."

I tried to remember if the girls had joined in the conversation at all, but nothing came to mind. Regardless, Amelia had been there at the table and had certainly heard our conversation. And now she was mysteriously out of hand sanitizer and Amy Blankenship was seriously ill. There couldn't be a connection, could there? I was probably imagining things. But then I recalled the yellow feather in her journal, and I knew anything was possible.

# CHAPTER FORTY-EIGHT

I'd managed to get a few hours of sleep sometime after two, but it hadn't been restful. I awoke groggy and out of sorts. It took me a minute or two to remember why I'd had such a bad night.

"Don't get all agitated," I muttered. "Maybe Amy is fine. Maybe she—" I looked around guiltily to see if Dan had caught me talking to myself, then realized I could hear the water running. He was in the shower, thank goodness. I was going to have to pull myself together if I was going to accomplish anything today. First on my list was checking on Amy's condition. I'd have to be surreptitious about getting the information. I didn't want to draw any unnecessary attention to either Amelia or myself.

Breakfast that morning caused shockwaves. I plopped two boxes of cold cereal on the table, along with a gallon of milk. My family stared at me in disbelief. Cold cereal was usually reserved as a nighttime snack. I always cooked a hot breakfast.

"Well? Get started. I have a lot on my schedule today." I turned and left the dining room. I could hear Dan asking the girls which kind of cereal they wanted and helping them to fill their bowls. As I headed for the stairs, Mama's door opened. She was fully dressed in one of her appropriate outfits.

"Jess, I need a favor."

I stopped. "Yes?"

"I need to get to that attorney's office today, and I don't have cab fare."

I looked at her stonily. "I didn't know you had another appointment."

"I don't. But after waiting around for him to call me back and getting bubkes, I decided I'm just going to go there and plant myself in his waiting room. He can't disrespect me like this," she said indignantly.

The last thing I cared about was Mama's hurt feelings. This was not the time for me to have to deal with her.

"Go ahead and take two twenties out of my purse. Will that be enough?"

"I think so. Maybe I should borrow your credit card, just in case?"

I said nothing, just looked at her. She bustled out of her room and made for the hall table where I always placed my purse.

"Never mind, I'm sure. If the cabby demands more, I'll handle it somehow."

The girls and I were out of the house before Dan had even finished dressing for work. A sense of urgency was driving me forward. I had to get to school and find out Amy's status.

"Mama, why are we in such a rush?" grumbled Amelia. "We're going to be at school way too early." Amanda and Abigail nodded their heads in agreement as I scooted them out the door and into the car.

"I have a meeting," I said. It wasn't exactly a lie. I was planning on waylaying the nurse as soon as possible.

There was blessedly little traffic so we got to our destination in record time. After depositing the girls at their before-school care facilities, I rushed into the front office.

"Where's Doris?" I asked the secretary in a pseudo-calm manner. "I wanted to thank her again for being so kind to Amelia yesterday."

"She called and said she's going to be late. She was at the

hospital last night with Amy."

"How is Amy?" I asked with just the right note of concern.

"Oh, she's going to be fine, from what I understand." The secretary lowered her voice. "It turns out her sickness was self-inflicted, if you know what I mean." She raised her hand to her mouth in a drinking motion.

"Oh, surely not. She's so good at her job. To come to school impaired—well, that just boggles my mind."

The secretary, Minna, nodded sagely. "You know what they say about psychologists. They only go into that line of work to try and fix their own problems."

Even though I agreed with that statement, I shook my head sadly. "Well, let's hope she gets the help she needs. And Minna, could you buzz me when Doris gets in? Or ask her to come by my room?"

"Sure. Sorry, I have to take this call." She gave me a brief wave as I left the office.

I was in agony all morning. I'd had no word of Doris, and I desperately needed to talk with her. There were some gaps in the story that only she could fill. I gave the students extra seat work to keep them busy and quiet, but still found myself pacing up and down the aisles, looking over their shoulders as they labored away.

I'd just returned to the classroom after walking the students to art when Doris came rushing up.

"Hi, Jess, Minna said you wanted to talk with me. It's been a crazy morning. I didn't get in until ten, and then there was a vomiter and an asthma attack. Is something wrong? How's Amelia?" She stopped to catch her breath, putting her hand against her bountiful chest.

"I wanted to thank you for helping Amelia yesterday. She's fine—there's nothing to worry about. I was wondering about something, though." I paused and the nurse looked at me expectantly.

"It's just . . . well . . . do you know what Amelia was doing in Amy's office? Why she wasn't in class?"

"Oh, she wasn't *in* the office, dear. She was in the hall outside of it. Apparently Amy saw her and asked if she could fill her water bottle from the fountain in the hall. Amelia did, they talked for a few seconds, and then Amy collapsed. Amelia came straight to get me. She's really something. So mature and self-possessed for her age. You must be so proud of her."

"Yes, she's really something," I replied, not meeting Doris' eyes. "By the way, I heard you were at the hospital last night. Is Amy going to be okay?"

Doris suddenly looked nervous. Now she was avoiding my eyes. "I believe she's going to take some time off. I really can't say anything more—confidentiality, you know. If there's nothing else Jess, I'd better scoot back to my office. No rest for the wicked, ha-ha." Giving my hand a good-bye squeeze, she was gone.

I sat down hard in my chair as though my bones had turned to mush. Leaning over my desk, I clutched my head in my hands. No rest for the wicked. The phrase had an ominous meaning to me. I wasn't the wicked one, and yet I was the person under stress. It was another example of the inequities that had always plagued my life.

# CHAPTER FORTY-NINE

After an interminable afternoon, it was finally time to go home. I was silent on the drive, planning my next move. I needed to confront both Amelia and Mama and get some answers before I knew how best to handle things. The girls could tell that I was in no mood for nonsense so they remained quiet.

When we pulled up to the house I got out without a word and went straight to my room. I could hear the girls chattering to each other downstairs but managed to tune them out. I stretched out on my bed and closed my eyes, breathing slowly and deeply. I needed to be calm and in control. If my assumptions were correct, about both Mama and Amelia, the consequences needed to be sure and final.

After about twenty minutes, I sat up. I was ready. I could hear Mama's voice coming up the stairwell. She sounded agitated. This could be the perfect time go eyeball-to-eyeball with her. She tended to say more than she meant to when she was upset.

As I came down the stairs I almost ran into Mama. She was just starting up, apparently looking for me.

"There you are! I've been looking all over for you! While you've been having a nice nap, I've been in such a state! That SOB of a lawyer is a crook! I'll have him disbarred! I'll—"

I raised a hand to stop her verbal barrage. "Hold on, Mama. Let's go sit in the living room and you can tell me what's going on. Where are the girls?"

"Eating their snack. Wait till you hear what happened!" She kept talking as we entered the living room. I sat on the wing chair, leaving the couch for her. Sitting in a higher position gave me an advantage.

"I know what Teddy wanted. He wanted me to be taken care of, no matter what. That's why he wrote that will. But that shyster is trying to say that my sweet Teddy came to see him with some song-and-dance about having doubts about me, thinking I hadn't been honest with him."

"Well, Mama, that's not really inaccurate, is it? Had you told him about your prison record?"

"No, but I was going to! I knew he'd accept me. He loved me!" Tears were rolling down her face, but I was unmoved. I'd viewed this scene before.

"Just what exactly did Mr. Blankenship say?"

"He said the holographic will was overridden by Teddy's conversation with him. He said I wouldn't get a penny—nothing! Not the house, or the boat—nothing!"

"So all your hard work didn't pan out, did it? Getting Teddy to write the will, pretending you didn't know he was going to confront you about your past that last night. I have to admire your skill in handling the police. I don't know if I could have been as believable if I had just killed a man."

"I've always been able to reel in men. They want to believe a pretty woman." She had a self-satisfied look on her face. "You've got that ability, too, Jess. I've seen you play Dan like a fiddle."

I stiffened but said nothing, waiting for her to implicate herself further.

"Not that I did anything wrong, of course," she added hastily. "Teddy's death was an accident, just like I said."

"Like Matt? And Daddy? And—"

"Oh, stop harping on the past! They were no good anyway! The world's a better place with those two gone. And if Teddy

226

had just been as honorable as he pretended, he'd be sitting right here beside me, instead of lying in a cold grave." She buried her face in her hands, crying in earnest now.

I'd heard enough. She'd as good as confessed. When I stood up and left the room, she didn't even seem to notice. I was on a roll. Now it was Amelia's turn.

Walking into the kitchen, I saw my three daughters sitting at the table, munching zucchini cookies and gulping milk. They looked so precious, so innocent. I wanted to believe the best, I truly did. But I had a job to do.

"Mama, why's Gr—I mean, Aunt Mae crying?" Amelia looked up at me with clear, guilt-free eyes.

"Let's go up to your room and talk about it. You're through with your snack, aren't you?"

She nodded and helped me take the platter and glasses to the sink. She looked surprised that I just left the dishes there without rinsing them off and putting them into the dishwasher.

"Girls, you may watch *Happy House* while Amelia and I are talking. As soon as it's over, get started on your reading logs."

"Yay! Thanks, Mama!" Abigail hugged my legs as Amanda jumped up and down in glee. They raced out to the family room.

Once in Amelia's room, I waited for her to get settled on her bed, then dragged her desk chair beside it. I sat down and looked at her, hoping that I was wrong in my suspicions.

"I don't really want to talk to you about Grandma. We have something else to discuss."

"What, Mama?"

"You haven't been honest with me, have you? You didn't tell me about filling Ms. Blankenship's water bottle for her." I waited for her reply.

After a few uncomfortable moments, she sat up and looked defiantly at me.

"I didn't do anything wrong! She was always looking at me, trying to get me in trouble! I just thought she'd get a tummy-ache or something! Besides, my teacher told the class that she was going to be okay. So it's no big deal, right, Mama?" she wheedled.

I stood up and pushed the chair back to the desk. "You'll stay in your room tonight. I'll bring your dinner up to you."

"But Mama—" she wailed. I didn't look back.

When Dan came home, I simply told him Amelia was being punished for not turning in her assignments in school. He accepted that, probably because he was distracted by Mama. She'd pounced on him with her tale of woe as soon as he came in.

"Now, Mae, it doesn't really sound like Blankenship did anything wrong. I don't think you have grounds to go to the bar association."

"But Dan, he treated me so shabbily! Like, like I was some gold digger or something."

"He was probably just distracted. You know his wife was rushed to the hospital yesterday. She collapsed at school." He looked at me. "Honey, didn't you hear about that? You didn't mention it."

"It must have slipped my mind. I barely know her." I walked mechanically into the kitchen and began to prepare dinner. I could still hear Mama, somewhat calmer now, and Dan's low, rumbly voice soothing her. He was a good man. I knew I could trust him to always try to do the right thing.

I made it through the rest of the evening, God knows how. I pleaded grading and paperwork and retreated to the living room. Dan, Mama, and the two little ones watched TV together after homework had been checked. The only time I interacted with the family was briefly at the dinner table, although I didn't eat. When I took Amelia's meal to her, she turned her head to the wall, and I breathed a sigh of relief that I didn't have to speak with her.

Eventually it was bedtime. I let Dan take over storytelling duties and dragged myself upstairs. Just before I closed my eyes, a stray thought flitted through my brain. The rope was unraveling, and I would soon be free. My sleep that night was dark and dreamless.

# CHAPTER FIFTY

"I'm not going to school today," I told Dan as I was blow-drying my hair. "I forgot that I have my annual physical today. I had to reschedule it, remember? It seemed easier just to take the whole day off."

"Oh yeah, sure," replied Dan distractedly. I knew he had no clue, but that was okay. The fewer questions the better.

This morning's breakfast was a far cry from yesterday's. I made strawberry waffles with whipped cream. I felt as light as the whipped cream myself, with all my troubles floating away. No one really complimented me, but I could tell my efforts were appreciated by the way the plates were almost licked clean.

After breakfast I calmly helped the girls gather their belongings and finish all of their last-minute preparations. I told Mama I'd be coming back after I took them to school. She just nodded and informed me that she was going back to bed. "Yesterday completely devastated me, and I need to rejuvenate myself" was how she put it.

I gave Dan an extra-big hug and a long kiss. He came out of it gasping for air but with a huge smile on his face. "Wow, maybe I should take the day off, too," he joked.

I patted his cheek. "I know you've got a busy day, sweetie. Just remember that I love you."

The girls and I had a pleasant drive to school. We chatted, laughed, and even sang a verse of "The Wheels on the Bus." I waved good-bye and pulled out of the school parking lot. Amelia in particular looked so happy, it warmed my heart. She'd been in such a foul mood last night after our chat, I was glad she was having a good start to her day.

I spent a little bit of time driving aimlessly through our town. We'd been content here. It was a great place to raise a family. In fact, it was just the type of place I'd dreamed of living when I was a girl. It was quite an accomplishment, and one that I was very proud of, to have moved from the dusty streets of Needles to this green and lovely town.

Stopping by the drugstore, I picked up the prescription refill I'd phoned in. With any luck, Dan wouldn't realize his Ambien had been refilled until much later. I headed for home with a light heart.

Mama was up and watching daytime TV when I got home. She was wearing an old terrycloth robe that I didn't even realize she owned and her hair was caught up haphazardly in a metal clip. She looked up forlornly when I came in.

"Mama, Mama," I said, shaking my head, "you mustn't let yourself go like this. So things didn't work out with Teddy. So what? You've always managed to pick yourself up and move on."

She looked startled at my kindness. "You're right, dear girl, but I just felt like I needed some down time, you know?"

"What if we go out to lunch today? I'll even pull Amelia out of school. I know she'd love it."

"Really?" Mama sounded suspicious. "I thought there was nothing more important in your mind than school and following rules."

I shrugged. "I guess I'm just in a funny mood today. Don't look a gift horse in the mouth. Isn't that what you always say?"

She laughed delightedly. "That's my girl! Now, where are we going? Should I dress up, or go for a casual look?"

We chatted for a minute about possible restaurants and then she hurried off to change. Once she was safely in her room I picked up the phone and called my school.

"Hi, Minna, this is Jess. I'm going to have to take Amelia out of school. Her grandmother is quite ill, and I need her with me. No, not Dan's mother—my mother. Oh, you didn't? Yes, she's been staying here. Anyway, I'll be by in about thirty minutes. I'd appreciate it if you could have her waiting in the office for me. Thanks." I clicked off the phone and stood still for a moment. My plan was in effect now. It was no longer just a hypothetical notion. I realized that I felt more serene and in control than I had in a long time.

Mama came out in a bright pink and green capri set. "What do you think?" she asked, making a model turn.

"Very cute," I nodded. "I was just going to make myself a cup of tea. Would you like one?"

"Yes, but remember to put in plenty of sugar. You know that's the way I like it. Now, if I can just do something with this hair." She tugged at her bangs and went back into her room.

I put the water on to boil and then went upstairs to my bathroom. An almost full bottle of Vicodin was in the medicine chest, left over from when I'd had oral surgery last year. It was a bit ironic that Dan had actually prescribed it. I had taken one or two pills, but quickly decided I'd rather be in pain than feel out of control. I shook the bottle in my hand, then put it in my pocket and went back down to the kitchen.

I caught the kettle just before it began to whistle. I hate that noise. Humming, I fixed two cups of tea—mine plain, no milk or sugar, and Mama's loaded with sugar and my special ingredients. I giggled to myself. Mama didn't like alcohol or medication much, but today she'd get a nice double dose of painkillers and sleeping aids. It was really a kindness. She'd find everything so much more peaceful.

I took her tea into her room. She was seated at her dressing table, still fussing with her hair. "Here you go, Mama, just the way you like it, nice and sweet. I'm going to go pick up Amelia. I'll be back in a jiff."

"Okay, sweetie. I'll be ready when you get back." She leaned into the mirror and began putting on her mascara.

"Don't let your tea get cold."

She grimaced. "Ugh, there's nothing worse than cold tea!" She picked up the cup and took a hearty sip. "Tastes wonderful. Thank you."

I waved and left her room. It had all been easier than I'd expected. Mama was always so ready to believe that she was in the driver's seat, that no one could put anything over on her. She was sadly mistaken this time.

I turned the radio on as I drove to the school to pick up Amelia. Somehow I didn't want to be alone with my thoughts.

Amelia was waiting in the office, full of questions. "Why are you taking me out of school, Mama? Am I in trouble? Is something wrong?"

I smiled indulgently as we walked out to the car. "No, sweetie, nothing like that. I just thought that with everything that's been going on, it would be fun to have a little treat. You and Grandma and I are going out to lunch."

Amelia's eyes widened, first with pleasure, then with apprehension. "It's not going to be like at the tea house, is it?"

"No, no." I laughed. "Grandma and I made up. Everything's fine. Hey, want to stop and get a strawberry-banana mixup at the drive-in? We've got plenty of time."

"Really, Mama? That's my favorite drink! Gee, thanks."

We pulled up to the drive-in. There was already a line, even though it wasn't noon yet.

"Sweetie, I'm going to run in and get it. It'll be faster. You wait here."

Amelia nodded, her face eager with anticipation. I was completely prepared. I'd pulverized the pills before I left the house and had them in a Baggie in my purse. After ordering and paying for the drink, I ducked into the restroom and added my special touch.

"Here you go. Enjoy. Better drink it up before we get home or Grandma will want one, too, and we'll never get to the restaurant." We both laughed, and Amelia gladly slurped the fruity drink.

I drove home slowly, glancing back at Amelia in the rearview mirror. It didn't take very long before her eyelids drooped and her head began to loll. I pulled over and took the drink out of her hand before it spilled on the car seat. No need for this to be a messy undertaking.

When we got to the house I pulled into the garage. I knew it would be tricky getting Mama into the car, and I didn't need any nosy neighbors wondering what was going on. Leaving Amelia in the car, I hurried into the house.

"Mama? Mama, I'm home. Are you ready?" No answer. That was good. It meant things were working according to plan. I almost tiptoed to her room.

She was slumped over her dressing table, breathing heavily. I frowned when I noticed her tea had spilled on the carpet. I resisted the urge to clean it up. There just wasn't time.

I quickly stripped the comforter from her bed and laid it on the floor. I pushed and shoved Mama onto the spread, then grabbed the ends so she was cocooned inside. Luckily she was smaller than me. I began to drag her through the house and into the garage.

It was harder than I thought it would be—not physically, but emotionally. Seeing Mama so vulnerable was a first for me. I wasn't sure how it made me feel. I shook off such thoughts and concentrated on getting her into the car.

Finally I was ready. Mama was in the backseat with Amelia. Both their faces looked so sweet in repose, it was hard to believe they were capable of such evil. I sighed. Unfortunately, as I knew all too well, they were. And nothing would change them. That's why what I was doing was the only right thing.

I drove sedately through town, but picked up speed once I was on the open highway. I knew exactly where I was going. There was a turn-off up ahead that led to the lake. People had been railing against the road as a danger for years. It was narrow and steep, and one of the curves had been the scene of several accidents, some of them fatal. In fact, it had such a bad reputation, I had never allowed Dan to use it. When we went to the lake, we took the long way there. It added almost an hour to the trip, but it was safer.

I almost felt like someone else was driving. My foot pressed down on the accelerator, and dispassionately I watched the speedometer climb. This would work; it had to. I'd loaded the trunk with four full cans of gas yesterday. That ensured there would be nothing left.

The sign ahead said "Dangerous Curve." Praying that it told the truth, I steered straight for the guard rail.

# CHAPTER FIFTY-ONE

Daddy brought me my journal so I'd have something to do. He would never look in it, not like Mama. She was always so suspicious. I guess I was right not to trust her. The doctors said if I hadn't been thrown from the car, I might have died, too. They still had to pump my stomach though—ugh.

Now it's just me and Daddy and Amanda and Abigail. That's okay. They all treat me real good, especially since I'm in the hospital. My leg is broken and I've got lots of scrapes and scratches. The nurses all act like I'm special. I can hear them whispering to each other when they think I'm asleep. They say that Mama was crazy. I don't think she was crazy, I just think she was a wuss. She was afraid of everything. I sort of miss her though—and especially Grandma. She was lots of fun.

When Daddy comes to see me, he has a real sad look on his face. He told me last night that I shouldn't worry, because Grandma Stranahan was going to move in to help take care of us. I started crying, and he hugged me.

"I know you miss your mom, baby. Don't worry. Everything is going to be all right."

I didn't tell him I was crying because I don't like Grandma Stranahan. She's even stricter than Mama. She always wants to be the boss. She'd better not try telling me what to do.

# ABOUT THE AUTHOR

**Valerie Benzley** is a first-time author who began writing seriously after her retirement five years ago. She worked as a special education teacher and school counselor for twenty-eight years and still enjoys working with children and adolescents as a substitute teacher. Valerie lives in Mesa, Arizona, near her two adult children. She enjoys writing, traveling, writing, volunteer work, writing, family and friends, and, of course, writing.